As Fate Would Have It

*Snowy Fate
*Sarah's Fate
*Mason's Fate

Marissa Dobson

Published by Sunshine Press

Printed in the United States of America

ISBN-13: 978-0-9886684-6-1

DEDICATION

To my wonderful husband who puts up with all my quirks.
Who else would listen to me brainstorm in the middle of
the night?

Contents

SNOWY FATE   2

Chapter One   2

Chapter Two   8

Chapter Three   16

Chapter Four   20

Chapter Five   26

Chapter Six   30

Chapter Seven   36

SARAH'S FATE   **40**

Chapter One   40

Chapter Two   46

Chapter Three   52

Chapter Four   58

Chapter Five   62

Chapter Six   68

Chapter Seven   72

Chapter Eight   76

Chapter Nine   82

Chapter Ten   88

Chapter Eleven   92

Chapter Twelve   96

Chapter Thirteen   102

Chapter Fourteen   106

MASON'S FATE   **110**

Chapter One   110

Chapter Two   116

Chapter Three   124

Chapter Four   128

Chapter Five   136

Chapter Six   140

Chapter Seven   144

Chapter Eight   152

Chapter Nine   158

Chapter Ten   164

Chapter Eleven   168

ABOUT THE AUTHOR   **171**

OTHER BOOKS BY MARISSA DOBSON   **172**

Snowy Fate

Chapter One

Looking out the window, the snow was coming down with such force Aspyn Layton couldn't even see her rented SUV that she left in the driveway a few hours before. The snowstorm was going to be one of the worst on record, and she was stuck in the heart of it. She tried to leave, get out of dodge before the storm hit, but all roads leaving town were closed. *I'm stuck in this house surrounded by all of his things,* she thought with disgust.

Of all the places in the world she didn't want to be in, this house was the top of her list. She didn't want to see her pictures he had on the mantle, or the journal he addressed to her. Those things just made her angry. If he cared so damn much, where was he all her life? If you really care for someone then you don't run away from them! No, you stay, even through the bad times.

Not the man who gave her life, her father. No, he ran; he ran as fast and as far as he could. What kind of father did that? Not one who cared, that was for sure.

She thought she was over this. So many times in her childhood she asked her mother, "Did daddy leave because I'm a bad girl?"

The answer was always the same. "No sweetie. You're not a bad girl. You're just a little different and your daddy couldn't handle it. But you got me. Isn't that enough?" Then Mom would get that sad look on her face and she would end up comforting her mother instead of the other way around.

It wasn't until she was a teenager that she realized how different she was. She knew things before they happened. She was faster and stronger than anyone she knew. Her mother finally broke down one day, telling her these abilities came from her father. That was when she realized how deep her resentment for her father ran. He was the one who passed on her abilities; causing her to be a freak among her friends. Instead of helping embrace the daughter he helped create, he left her mother and her to fend for themselves.

Now, to find out her mother sent him pictures and letters about her was unbelievable. She wanted to know why; but there was no one to ask. Her mother passed away a year before, and now he was dead. It was just her against the world.

Surrounded by his things, she had to face the memories of her childhood. Minute by minute her emotions changed. One minute she was filled with rage and the next she was disappointed that he would never see the women she turned out to be.

What would you have thought of the woman I became? she asked the empty room, as her eyes locked onto a picture of them shortly before he left. "You can't take any credit for the woman I became, but I wish you were here to see it," she said as the front door burst open.

* * *

She picked up the fire poker as she looked at the naked man before her. "Who are you?" Even though she was startled by the man who stood before her, she had a feeling that he meant her no harm. A man that sexy couldn't harm anyone; except to break a girl's heart. He looked as though he should be posing for *Playgirl* instead of standing in the cozy living room.

"The better question is who are you and what are you doing here?" he asked as he shook the wet snow off his body. He stood there, not the least bit concerned that he was naked, nor that he was wet from head to toe. Her heart was fluttering, and desire was heating her cheeks. She wanted to explore his toned body with her hands, and her tongue. His dark hair was wind blown into disarray; that served to make him look dangerous, and that much sexier.

"The name's Aspyn. Now who are you?"

"You're his daughter," he said more out of shock, then in question. "I'm Damon Andrews. John, your dad's lawyer, didn't think you would be coming to the house, or I would have left."

Once she heard this man was a friend of her father's, she quickly squashed the attraction that was building inside her. There was no way she could pursue someone who knew her father. She didn't want to know any more than she already did about the man who ran out on her and her mother.

"It wasn't the plan. I agreed to sell the place and his things. I planned to head straight home, but the storm rolled in, leaving me no time to get out of town. I didn't have anywhere else to go and I didn't think anyone was living here. The lawyer mentioned the key under the rug if I wanted to stop." She lowered the weapon as she spoke.

He nodded in understanding. "If there's anything of his you want, please feel free to take it. There are lots of pictures of you."

"He never gave me anything while he was alive and I don't want anything now." The first tear was threatening to fall.

"Hey there, I didn't mean to upset you. I'm sorry," he said, crossing the room in two strides.

"It's not you. It's just being here, around all this. It's more than I can handle now. I'm not a woman who cries at the drop of the hat, I don't know what is wrong with me. All the years he missed, and now it's too late. This is like crying over spilled milk."

He gently laid a hand on her shoulder. "He wouldn't want you to be upset. He did what he thought was right when you were a child. It might not have been the best decision, but he felt it was the only way. It was the only way to give you a semi-normal childhood, and he regretted that decision every day."

She looked him in the eye and with fire in her eyes, she lashed back. "I know this is going to sound childish and ungrateful, but then he should have come back for us." She shook off his hand. "But none of that matters now, it's too late. What are you doing here? Better yet, why are you naked?"

Taking a step back, he nodded to the cot made in the corner. "I've been staying with your father. I'm building a house on the other side of the lake and was living at the hotel. On your dad's better days, he would come over and helped with the construction. The heat and plumbing aren't finished yet because of the freezing weather. Your dad invited me to stay until it was finished. When he passed and I found out you didn't want the house, I put the offer in to buy it. I couldn't see it sold off to someone who wouldn't appreciate the beauty of the area. As for my lack of clothing, well that is a long story. Why don't I make us something to eat? I'm sure you're starving."

"That would be great."

"On one condition…you must read your father's journal. You need to understand why. It will affect you more than I can explain." Before she could object he added, "Please. There's stuff in there that you really need to know. I told him time and time again that he needed to find you before it was too late and tell you. But he didn't listen. The first page is all I am asking. After that, if you don't want to read any more, I won't pester you anymore *today*."

Chapter Two

From her father's bedroom, she could hear Damon
moving around in the kitchen. *One page*, she told herself.
Why she felt the need to listen to him was beyond her.
Maybe deep down she really wanted to read it and just
needed an excuse.

The pictures of her continued in the bedroom, the
most recent one of her graduating college was on the
bedside table, next to the journal Damon mentioned. It
was a dark brown leather journal, well-worn, and if the
page marker was any indication, was almost full.

Picking up the journal, she felt a lump rise in her
throat, and her stomach was doing flip flops.

August 14, 1995

*Today I made the hardest decision of my life…I left Aspyn in
her mother's care. I can't be the father she needs me to be and protect
her. My enemies will hurt her just to get back at me. Her mother will*

take good care of her and alert me if there's a threat. This is the only way I can be sure she is safe.

I had to get in my car and drive away even as I watched her cry on the porch steps and beg me not to leave. She doesn't understand now. But someday, somehow I will see that she understands.

There might not be a daddy handbook, but if there was, the first thing in there would be to protect your child at all cost. That is what I did today.

* * *

She laid the journal on the bed as the memory of that day washed over her. That day she felt as if her world was ending. The day before, was so perfect. He took her to the park and spent all day playing with her. He always made her feel like she was the center of his world, so special and loved. Waking up the next morning, she went to find him, only to overhear him talking to her mother.

Her eyes closed as the scene played before her.

"Amy, I'm doing the only thing I can. I can't ask you and Aspyn to live like this any longer. You need to be safe, and with me around, you can't be. I'll find this guy and when I do, I'll return to you and Aspyn. It won't be long."

Her mother was sitting at the kitchen table, crying into her coffee cup, still in her pajamas and her hair muddled from sleep. "What will you tell Aspyn? She is just a little girl and you're going to break her heart. She won't understand."

"Someday I'll make her understand. She's our world. You wouldn't want something to happen to her because of me. Try to explain things to her until I get back."

That was when they caught sight of her standing in the corner. She might have only been five, but she knew things were about to change. Seeing her there, watching them fight, it brought more tears to her mother's eyes. Her mother lowered her head, silently crying, and her father seemed locked in place until he dragged his hand over his face and through his hair. She remembered he did that when he was upset or nervous.

"Darling, Daddy has to go away for a little while. I'll try to be back soon. Until then, be a good girl for your mommy. I love you." He bent down and kissed her before picking up his bag and heading for the door.

"Daddy, don't go!" She ran behind him. But he didn't stop. Her mother yelled for her to come back into the kitchen but she didn't listen. She wanted her father. She stood on the porch crying and screaming for him to stay with her as the car backed down the driveway.

As quickly as the memory came, it was over, but the tears and heartbreak remained.

* * *

"Aspyn, dinner's ready," Damon called from the other room.

She wiped away the tears from her cheeks, grabbed the journal and headed to the kitchen. Damon was right. One page and she would want to read more. Reading his journal didn't mean she forgave him. She was a long way from that, but she wanted to know more about the man that ran out on her. She wanted to know he felt the same agony from the decision that she did.

She entered the kitchen just in time to see him dishing the food onto the plates. The kitchen suited the house with handmade cabinets, a stone top counter, and room for a small dining table. She was never much for formal dining rooms and always believed in eating in the kitchen. To her, eating in the kitchen reminded her of family and special times that should always be remembered. It was nice that her father had the same in his house. Was that one way they were like each other? How else were they alike?

"I see you took my advice," he said, nodding to the book.

"You knew about this? About his enemy? Did he ever find him?"

"Let the journal tell the story. I could never do it justice. Your father documented everything for you to read because he knew in the end it would be what you needed. It's what he would have needed. He said you were like two peas from the same pod."

"I don't know about that. Since he was never around, I doubt he would know, either."

"I wouldn't say he was never around." When she opened her mouth to ask what he meant, he held up his hand. "That's all I'm saying. All the answers you seek are in that book. You just have to be open and ready to accept them."

Placing the journal on the counter, she grabbed the plates to carry to the table. "I'll get drinks. What do you want?"

"Thanks. I'll take a beer from the fridge. Help yourself to anything in there."

She grabbed two beers, then used the corner of her sweater to twist off the caps before handing one to him. "Let's stop talking about my father for once. Tell me about you."

"There's not a whole lot to tell. I was traveling through the area, and took the wrong road. I fell in love with the area and haven't left. A few months ago, I bought the piece of land and starting building. My brother lives in the next county over. He owns a construction business and gets a lot of work in this area, so I've been working for him since settling down here."

"It's interesting for a single man to talk about settling down, that's unheard of where I'm from. My roommate has been dating the same man for five years and can't even get him to commit to living together."

With a smirk on his face. "Who said I was single?"

She dropped her fork, and it clattered to the plate. "Oh...I'm...sorry. I just thought..."

Laughter erupted from deep inside his chest, as he waved his hand in front of him. "I'm just messing with you. I couldn't help myself. Sorry." He gave her a large smile that made his eyes glow with happiness.

She had the sudden desire to throw something at him but instead gave him a dirty look.

"Hey, you're the one who jumped to the conclusion I was single."

"You're living here on a cot at my father's. If you had a wife, I suspect you would be living somewhere more acceptable," she said as she tried to figure him out. Since meeting him he seemed so serious, but now she realized there was a playful side as well.

"I can see the California way in you. You think you're better than everyone else."

"I'm not better than anyone. I was just saying you wouldn't be living with my father if you were married, now, would you?"

"You're probably correct there. So tell me about yourself." While he was waiting for her to fill him in on her life, he dug into the grilled chicken he cooked.

"There isn't much to tell. I recently graduated from college, and I'm still looking for a job. I have no family, just a few friends back home in California."

Between mouthfuls he asked, "What's your degree in?"

"Elementary education. I love children. It seemed the perfect fit for me." Talking about herself always made her uncomfortable, and instead of eating, she was nibbling. She was surprised at what a good cook he was.

"There just happens to be an opening here at the elementary school."

She had just taken a bite and nearly choked on her food. "No way! I'm not staying here. Once the weather is better, I'm leaving."

"You might come to like this area. Keep an open mind. We are going to be stuck here together for a few days. The snow isn't letting up anytime soon." He winked at her, with a big grin on his face.

* * *

After they finished dinner and loaded the dishwasher, she wanted to read more of the journal, but didn't want to be rude. While she was trying to approach the subject carefully, he leaned against the counter, taking a swig from his beer.

"I have some work to do. This would be a great chance for you to read more of the journal. I'll be in your father's office if you need me. The warmest place would be to curl up by the fire. It's going to get mighty cold tonight."

She smiled back at him. "It's like you read my mind. I really do want to read more."

Chapter Three

A few hours later, Damon was still in the office when she reached the part she believed was a joke. Not in her wildest dreams did she believe that there were shapeshifters in real life. That was something for movies and books. Not real life. Leaving the nice fire, she sought out the office.

"How dare you and my father turn this into some senseless joke!" she screamed. The resentment was burning through her.

He sat there, not answering as she continued on.

"This might be fun and games to you, Damon. But this is my life you're screwing with. You almost had me feeling sorry for him. Then I read this." She tossed the journal at him with the bookmark holding the place. "Go on—read it! Or do you already know what he wrote? Were you in on this joke from the beginning?"

He didn't bother opening the journal. "I haven't read it, but I'm sure I know what it says. Aspyn, it isn't us that's pulling this cruel joke on you, it's heredity and nature. You must have noticed you're different."

"Don't you dare go there! All my life my mother said my father left because I was different. All my life I wanted everyone to think I was normal." The anger she was feeling was still there in full force, but it was tinged with sadness.

"Aspyn, darling, I never said it was a bad thing. Being unique is something special. Let me explain."

"There's nothing you can do to make me believe it. The words in the journal are nothing but a fairytale. It isn't reality. I don't live in a fantasyland like my father did. Maybe he was ill." She turned to leave. She might not be able to get out of town, or even this house, but she didn't have to be in the same room with a man who was as demented as her father.

She didn't even make it two steps before he shoved her against the wall. He growled in her ear before saying, "Oh, I think I can make you believe it. You need to listen to me. If I have to tie you down until you hear me out, I will."

She tried to wiggle out of his grasp, but his hold was too strong. His arms held her like iron bars closed firmly around her. She couldn't get away. She realized that if he wanted to hurt someone, he would be able to easily. Even

17

with the fear rising up her spine, she couldn't help but notice that he was even sexier when he was angry. "Listen, I don't care. My father was a nut job, and I want nothing to do with it. I have a life back in California and I plan to get back to it soon. Until then, I hope we can just stay out of each other's way."

"That isn't going to happen. Not until you know the full story. Then, if you want me to go my own way, I will. Don't you even think it was odd I came back naked; especially in this weather?"

"Yes. But if you want to get pneumonia, that's your choice."

"I went for a run in my true form. When I returned, I saw the smoke from the fire you started and changed back. I had two choices: to come in as I was and scare you, or naked. Naked seemed to be the best option."

She leaned her head back against the wall and let out a sigh. She wanted to roll her eyes, but when dealing with crazy people that tends to make things worse. "Really? And what is your *true* form?" she asked in a mocking tone.

"Guess I should have come in like I was." With that, he lowered to the ground. Short, golden hair started to form all over his body. His clothes ripped and fell to the floor as his body started to change and morph.

His toned, six foot frame had transformed into the fierce mountain lion standing before her. Instead of being six foot in height, he was seven feet long, nose to tail, weighing around two hundred pounds. Before she could stop herself, a scream escaped her throat as she moved towards the door. Not wanting to give her back to the animal, she crept across the wall.

She was inches from the door frame when the mountain lion struck out his paw, catching the edge of the door and slamming it shut. Then, just like that, he was back in his human form, rising slowly from the crouched position to stand naked before her.

"Darling, does that change your opinion?"

Sliding down the wall to sit on the floor as her legs gave out, she replied, "I don't understand...none of this is possible."

He lowered himself to the floor to sit in front of her. "Darling, I know it's a lot to take in. But it's possible. You just saw it with your own eyes." His southern drawl was present in his words.

Chapter Four

They sat there in silence for a long while. She had her eyes closed and her head resting against the wall. He remained silent next to her, giving her the time she needed to adjust.

"Aspyn, you might not believe all this, but it's true. My animal knows you're my mate. You're the one I have been waiting for. The reason I came to this area. The day I took the wrong road and ended up here at the lake was the day fate put me on the path to find you. I could sense I would find my mate here. I had to settle down and stop traveling the world on a whim. I had to prepare myself to be the mate you need. Fate has decided we're ready for each other, and brought us together."

"It's been a long day and I need time to think. I know what my eyes saw, but my mind isn't ready to accept that. I'm going to bed."

"I'll let you have tonight, but tomorrow we'll have to deal with this. Night, Darling."

* * *

Damon knocked on her door early the next morning. She heard him moving around but wasn't ready to face him. Instead, she stayed in bed, not willing to face the day before her. She knew that weird things were going on here, and she wanted no part of them. But the snow was still coming down; abandoning any plans she had for a quick escape. He might be a mountain lion, but that didn't mean she wanted any part of it.

"Come in," she tried to say in a sleepy voice, but she failed miserably.

"I thought you would enjoy a nice hot breakfast and some strong coffee." He placed the tray in front of her in bed. "I heard you up most of the night. There's plenty more coffee."

"Thank you." She was surprised by how much breakfast in bed could affect her. She never had someone make her breakfast before, let alone serve it to her in bed. She was the one that was always doing for others, not the other way around. "It's always hard sleeping in a new place. Especially here with everything…" Instead of trying to explain, she picked up a forkful of omelet.

Sitting on the edge of the bed in loose fitting plaid pajama pants, and his bare chest with dark curls that drew her attention. "We need to discuss what happened last night." His voice was mild, but insistent.

21

"There's nothing to discuss."

"I think there is. You still don't understand."

"Oh, I understand just fine. I might not completely understand what happened to you last night, but it doesn't matter. I came here to sign some papers for my father's house, and take care of his will. Now I have done that, I will be returning to California. Whatever happened to you last night—I don't care. I don't care if you drugged my food last night so I thought I saw a mountain lion. All I care about it getting back to my life."

"Aspyn. Your father was a great man. I wish you could open your mind a little and accept that there are things you don't know. Things like what you saw last night are possible. If you keep living your life like this, you're going to live a pretty crappy existence."

"How dare you! You know nothing about me." Her voice was as cold as ice water.

"Oh, I know enough." His voice was laced with sarcasm. "More than you think I do." When she didn't take the bait, he continued. "You emotions are very clear to me. There's nothing you can hide from me. I knew from the second I walked through the door you were drawn to me. You couldn't take your eyes off me and it wasn't because I was naked. There's a connection between us that you have never felt before. One that you'll never feel again. You need to embrace it."

She tried to keep her eyes off his chest, but she kept picturing running her hands over it, her fingers playing lightly with the curls as she cuddled closer to him. Her fantasies were dangerous. She needed to stay away from this man, not get any closer. "It doesn't matter what might have been between us. What matters is we're two different people, from two different worlds."

"We aren't that different."

The sarcasm was coming back to her. "Oh, really. You're a…"

"Mountain lion." He supplied for her. "Yes, but so was your father, and so are you."

"I was born in this form, as you call it, and have never changed. As for my father, I couldn't care less what he was or wasn't."

"Aspyn, you would have been born in that form, and as a woman, you would not go through the change until you found your mate."

"Then I guess I'll give up dating, because I don't want to be an animal."

"It's too late for that option. You already found your mate, and the change will happen soon."

She tried to laugh but it caught in her throat. *Was he serious?* she thought.

"Once you embrace me as your mate, the change will happen and your father's enemies will be after you instead of him."

"What makes you so certain you're my mate?"

"There's a glow around you. Some people would call it an aura. One that is only seen by your mate. Plus the connection between us, it's almost like two magnets trying to connect to each other. You must feel the energy in the air."

"I feel drawn to you. But you're a very attractive man. I doubt it has anything to do with this mating you are talking about."

Moving up the bed so he was closer to her, he reached out and brushed the side of her check. "My darling Aspyn, you're my mate. You're the reason I'm here. I want you to accept it. To let me claim you. I can protect you and provide for you. You must only accept me."

"If I don't? What happens then?"

"Then Darling, we'll remain unmated and live miserable lives. We will not find another mate until one of us dies." His weight lifted off the bed and he headed for the door. "I'm going for a run. I suggest you read the rest of the journal."

Chapter Five

The journal lay on the bedside table. He must have placed it there without her knowing. Her stomach felt as if it was in knots. She set the rest of the breakfast aside, eyeing the journal carefully. She wasn't convinced she wanted to read any more of it, but she couldn't stop herself from reaching for it.

My dearest daughter,

If you're reading this, it means one of two things; either you don't believe a word out of this old man's mouth, or I have passed on before I had the chance to tell you the whole story. One day you'll find your mate and you'll understand the love I have for your mother. Yes, I say have, because no matter how long we are apart, the love is still there as strong as ever. Your mother is my heart and soul. She's the reason I get up every day. I wish I could be with both of you.

Many years ago, I left you and your mother because of the hunters. They're after all shifters, they knew what I was. Staying with you and your mother would have put you both in danger. I thought I could protect you both, but in the end I knew I wasn't enough. Your mother refused to come home to my people. She wanted to give you a normal life; she didn't believe you were like me. But soon your abilities were hard to deny, even for her.

At a very young age, you were always in tune with people and their feelings. You are a natural caregiver. You also have intuition and will one day be able to embrace your telepathic skills. Those will come when you find your mate, but you're already working on honing that skill. You have used it on me a few times when I was unaware and I suspect you have used it on your mother without her knowledge. But the biggest ability that your mother can't deny is you're stronger than normal humans, and your emotions have the tendency to change at a drop of a hat.

The day that you accept your mate, you'll fully come into your gifts. You will then be able to shift forms at will. Women are protected from shifting forms until they're mated. This way, the mate can assist with this process.

Be sure to accept a mate who can protect you. Once you come into your gift, the hunters will know and they'll be after you. I killed the hunter that was after me all those years ago, but don't be fooled there are others just as vicious. That is why I couldn't return to your mother. The hunters would just follow me. I check in with her from time to time and would watch you from afar, but I could never risk you. You mean everything to your mother and me, and we have done this to protect you, not to hurt you. We have sacrificed our love so you *could be safe and live a reasonably normal life. Now it's time that you face your destiny. You mate is waiting…*

I have always loved you,

Your Father.

* * *

Reaching the end of the journal, she tried to wrap her head around what she'd just discovered. If her father was right, could she accept it? Was Damon her mate? What if she didn't want this life? The questions raced around her brain with no clear answers.

She paced the confines of the bedroom as she tried to come to a decision. She knew Damon would be back soon and would want to know her decision. Could she really put her life on the line? Deal with hunters on a regular basic? What about having children? Any children she had would be in danger as well. Was that something she was willing to risk?

What am I thinking? This is all crazy. You can't just turn into an animal on command, she scolded herself. She had to get out of here. She was snowbound at the worst possible time. Closing her eyes, she gave herself a pep talk; her thoughts were interrupted by her cell phone ringing.

The caller id said *Sarah Calling.*

Her best friend and roommate was calling to check up on her. They met in college and had been inseparable ever since. "Hello."

She lay across the bed listening to her friend. "I wish." She let out a puff before continuing. "This damn snowstorm has me stuck here. I'm at my father's place, dealing with Damon, and about ready to pull out my hair."

She chuckled at something her friend said as she continued to stare at the ceiling above her. "Oh, he's attractive, but I don't think I want to get involved with someone who was so close to my father. Plus he tells some crazy stories."

When her friend asked her what stories, all she said was, "You wouldn't believe me if I told you." She didn't want to get into them right now. When she was safe and sound back home, maybe she would tell her the full story.

Thankfully, before her friend could nag her, she heard the front door open. "Listen, Sarah. I have to go now. I hope the storm lets up and I can be on my way home soon. Until then, take care of Stormy for me." Talking to Sarah made her miss their kitten, Stormy. It was really Sarah's, but she had grown attached to the little furball.

Before she hung up the phone, she heard her friends parting words: "Live for the moment. Do something wild. You're in a new place, even if only for a short while. Live it up."

Chapter Six

Her friend's words were still ringing in her ears when Damon knocked on her bedroom door. "Come in."

He opened the door slowly, as if he wondered what he would find. "I just wanted to check to make sure you were okay." She was sure he was wondering how she had reacted to the rest of the journal.

She propped herself up on her elbows so she could look at him. She was taken aback by his body again. He could have been on the cover of *Playgirl*. His dark hair was still wet from the snow, his chest was toned and flat. She felt a wave of regret as she noted that before he sought her out, he threw on a pair of jeans. She didn't want to see an inch of his body covered. She wanted to be able to admire him. "I'm not sure okay is the word. But I haven't sent out a death threat on you...yet." Her lips curled up in a smile.

He stayed in the doorway, smiling. There was a hint of something in his eyes she couldn't quite place. "Well, thank you, Darling." His southern drawl made her picture him in tight jeans and a cowboy hat, getting her hotter than she was before. "I promise you would have regretted it if you did. No one can do for you like I can. Why don't you let me show you?"

The moment he opened the door, her body start reacting to him. She could feel her heart pick up its pace, her pussy moistened with desire, her nipples hardened with the longing for his lips to gently suckle them. Sarah said live for the moment; that's what she planned to do. In a few days, she would be back in California and would never have to see him again.

In a low seductive voice she said, "Come here."

He hesitated, as if suddenly unsure of himself. This is what he said he wanted. His body and soul had to crave her as much as she craved him.

"You talk a big game, but when it comes down to it, you chicken out?" she asked with a teasing tone.

Throwing caution to the wind, he lunged at her. "I'll deliver, don't you worry about that." He landed on top of her, forcing her to lie back against the bed again. He gently brushed a strand of her long brown hair away from her face, and gazed deeply into her eyes. "I plan to remove the pain in your eyes tonight, once and for all. I'll give you the world if you let me, Darling."

"I don't want the world. All I want right now is you."
She let all her reservations fall aside as she leaned in to kiss him.

Their lips met and the desire that was building inside of them engulfed them, making them think of nothing other than each other. She wanted to forget her doubts and live in the moment. If her world crashed down around her in the morning, she wanted it to be worth it.

Their kiss broke when he lifted her sweater over her head. His attention was diverted from her lips to her hard, dusky pink nipples, reaching out for attention. She watched him fondle her breast as his lips locked onto her nipple with tantalizing possessiveness.

While he was busy with her nipple, she worked her hands between them to his jeans. Her fingers worked the zipper down, freeing his shaft. She wanted to wrap her hand around it, but the confining space would not allow much movement.

"Soon, Darling, soon," he said as he unbuttoned her jeans, sliding them off, along with her vibrant red panties. She now lay before him, naked as the day she was born.

He wiggled out of his jeans before returning his attention to her. "My Darling, you're beautiful. You shouldn't hide it behind bulky sweaters."

She laughed. "I'm sure you say that to all the women."

"No, love, you're the only one. I don't know who hurt you in the past, but you need to let go so you can love again. You need to let me in."

He took his time showing her he was the man for her. Making sure every moment was special. He caressed every curve of her body, and her cheeks heated with desire.

It wasn't long before she took matters into her own hands. She drew her fingers through his hair and she used it to draw him closer. When their lips met, the burning passion sizzled through their bodies, her tongue exploring his mouth with a hunger that wouldn't be denied.

His body perched on top of her as she spread her legs wider, giving him the access that he wanted. She cried out with anticipation as his erection met her tender flesh. She was moments away from something that would change her life forever.

She could tell he was holding back, fighting his natural animal desires as his shaft slowly entered her wet and waiting core. "I'm trying to be gentle, but my animal wants control," he growled.

"There will be time for slow and gentle later." Her eyes closed as desire coursed through her body.

The air around them crackled as he slid completely in, his body partially covering her as he worked his way in and out of her warm center. She lazily ran her fingers up and down his chest and her heart danced with excitement.

Her body squirmed beneath him as she drew near her climax. He paused to kiss her, whispering his love for each part of her body. She realized he wanted to bring them both to climax together; to make their lovemaking last until the very end.

He watched as her impatience grew to explosive proportions before continuing to please her. The passion pounded the blood through her heart, chest and head, making her need his every touch. Once again they found the tempo that bound their bodies together, and waves of ecstasy throbbed through them.

The passion she felt rose in her like the fires of hell, clouding her brain. She abandoned herself to the whirl of sensations. Moments later, he slammed home one last time as they both cried out with release.

He slid off her to lie beside her. She cuddled close to him, their legs still intertwined. He kissed the top of her forehead before throwing a blanket over them. She laid her head on his shoulder.

Chapter Seven

The next morning, they woke to find the snow had finally stopped. Her desire to leave this place, to run as fast as she could, was also gone. Right now all she wanted was to snuggle next to Damon and let the world pass her by. Nothing seemed as desirable as it did yesterday; her need to rush back to California was gone. What did she have waiting for her there…nothing.

"You look like you're in deep thought. What's wrong?"

Her mouth curved into an unconscious smile before answering. "Nothing could be wrong with you by my side."

She pulled him closer to her, bringing their lips together for a long kiss. As their lips met, she arched her back and pulled away, screaming in agony.

"Aspyn, I didn't realize it would be so soon. Don't fight it; it will only make the pain worse." He held her arms, trying to keep her on the bed as she found the pain.

"What's…happening to me?" she said through clenched teeth as she fought not to scream.

"The change. You're embracing your new life…and me as your mate." The anxiety and frustration he was feeling was written on his face as he watched her in so much pain.

"I'm not ready…" Her screams broke off anything else she was going to say.

"Shhh, Darling. It will be over soon. Stop fighting it and things will be over quicker."

"I can't…" She fought against his body, digging her nails into his arms, her legs trying to push him away.

She could feel her body starting to change and shift into its new form. She must be close, because hair started to grow and Damon stepped back, giving her room.

Her screams turned into groans as she shifted. Moments later, the moans of pain died away, and there she could feel and picture herself as a mountain lion. She looked down at her paws and saw tawny colored hair. *She had paws!* she thought as she looked at him with amazement in her eyes.

"Aspyn, focus on changing back. You must focus on being back in your body. The shift will only take seconds and won't be as painful as the first time. Come on, Darling."

The waves of apprehension swept through her. "I know, Darling, but this time it will be painless. The first time is always the hardest. Trust me." His hand reached out to touch her head, giving it a gentle rub. "Just picture yourself back in your own body."

She shifted back to find herself laying the floor. Her body shivered with chills and fatigue, her muscles screamed from the strain, but instead of sleep, she wanted him. She reached for him, and he was there. He was quickly becoming her rock through thick and thin.

After he got her in bed, he brought her an aspirin. "You should rest. The first time can take a lot out of you."

Her eyes were heavy, and sleep tried to drag her in, but the questions filled her mind. "Now what?"

Kissing her cheek, he spoke. "You should rest and we can talk about it all later."

"I don't want to sleep. I want to know what happens next."

"Next…I convince you to stay with me. You have already accepted me as your mate or you wouldn't have gone through the shift. That's half the battle."

"How do you plan on doing that?" she asked with a sleepy voice.

Without looking away, he reached in the nightstand and pulled out a ring box. "Aspyn, I started to build a house here because I knew this was where I would find my mate. I had no idea it was you until you arrived, I just knew this area would bring me the woman I was supposed to spend the rest of my life with. Please do me the honor of being my wife." He opened the box to show a stunning princess cut diamond ring.

Her heart sang with delight as she accepted his proposal. "Yes."

As he placed the ring on her finger, his hand trembled, but the smile on his face made his eyes light up like a million stars.

Sarah's Fate

Chapter One

Letting out a deep breath, Sarah McMillan leaned against the car door. What was I thinking? she pondered to herself while taking in her surroundings. The quiet countryside was a complete change to the life she left back in California. The air was lighter and for the first time in her life, she heard honest-to-God, real birds chirping.

Six months ago, her best friend and roommate Aspyn Layton left California to attend to her dead father's estate and never returned. A blizzard hit, leaving her stuck in her father's cabin with a man she'd never met. That trip changed both of their lives forever. Now here Sarah was following her friend on this journey to the country.

"Sarah, you made it!" she heard Aspyn call. Turning away from the countryside, she saw her friend step out of the house. Love suited Aspyn. She had a glow about her, letting everyone know that she was in love. "It's so good to see you. How was your trip?"

"Long," she said, fighting to hide the yawn. As Aspyn strolled toward her, she ran a hand through her long, blonde hair trying to make herself presentable. Spending most of the last three days on the road, she hadn't bothered to put on makeup or do much with her hair. She loved to make long trips comfortably, as her thin cotton lounge pants and tank top clearly stated.

"Come in. Damon and his brother are inside finishing a few last-minute things to make your stay comfortable. They'll be done shortly. Until then, why don't we have a glass of wine and catch up?"

"Damon! Josh! Sarah's here." Aspyn entered the cabin she inherited from her father. "Once the guys are done, they'll get your stuff."

She nodded as she took in the cabin. The large, stone fireplace off to the right dominated the living room. The cozy cabin had everything she needed, but most importantly the space to figure out what she wanted to do. She needed a change from California, but she wasn't sure the country was for her. Maybe New York, Boston or even Pittsburgh.

"I know it's not much," Aspyn said as if she knew what Sarah was thinking. "Damon and I planned to remodel it, but when you agreed to come stay here for a while we did what we could to make it feel like a home for you."

"I appreciate what you and Damon did and for allowing me to stay here. I really do like it. It's just such a big change." Her thoughts were going faster than she could keep up. *Am I doing the right thing leaving behind everything I knew in California and moving here?* Aspyn seemed so happy here. *Could I find the peace that she has? My life is so mixed up now, I didn't know what I want anymore.*

"Oh, I remember that feeling all too well. Trust me, it won't take long to adjust. A little peace and quiet is just what you need."

She wanted to agree with her friend. After all, they'd known each other for so long that she hoped Aspyn knew what she needed, because she was lost. At one time, her life was on the right track...

"You're thinking about Cain."

Aspyn could read her like a book. "I can't help it. I don't understand. Everything changed so suddenly."

"I know, sweetie." Aspyn handed her a glass of wine. "But it's better that you found out now."

Her throat was tight with more unshed tears, and her voice refused to work. *Better to find out now?* Seven years in what she thought was a committed relationship, only to find he was a self-centered jerk.

"I'm glad you're finally here. You need a fresh start."

She didn't know what she would say; thankfully, she didn't have to say anything. Two men came into the living room.

"There you guys are. Sarah, this is my fiancé Damon, and his older brother—"

"I'm Josh. I'm not only the older brother, but I'm also the wiser one. It's a pleasure to meet you. I've heard a lot about you." Josh offered her his hand, sending her a smile that made her weak in the knees.

"Same to you." She took his large, calloused hand into hers, giving it a sturdy shake. Her gaze taking in the man before her. He stood at least six foot two, with a dark tan that only hours in the sun could give a person. His black mop of curls added a boyish look to his mature face, and his green eyes sparkled as they found hers.

"Sorry, I really must be going. I'll see you tomorrow, Damon," Josh said, heading for the door.

Aspyn slipped into Damon's arms. "Hun, could you bring in her suitcases from the car?"

"Sure." He kissed her forehead before heading out the door.

A smile lit her face as she watched Aspyn. It was good to see her friend happy and in love. She'd never had the love with Cain that Asypn had—it made part of her envy her friend.

Josh was worth this trip alone. The memory of his skin-kissed body was etched in her mind, bringing a quickening to her heart.

Chapter Two

An hour later Sarah was alone in the house, unsure what to do with herself. She unpacked her suitcase and settled in. Aspyn had already stocked the fridge and cabinets with her favorites. *How do people live with such boredom?* she wondered for the third time since Aspyn and Damon left.

This weekend was going to be a long one. Monday she would have to call to have the cable and Internet turned on. Until then what would she do to fill her time?

The ringing doorbell jolted her out of her thoughts. *Aspyn?*

Opening the door, she found Josh standing in the rain on the other side. "Josh?" she asked, her voice full of surprise. *What is he doing here?*

"I didn't mean to bother you. I got home and realized I left my cell in the office."

"Oh sure, come in. I haven't been into the other bedroom, so I didn't realize it." She stepped back, giving him room to enter the cabin.

"You haven't gone into the office?" His eyes widened with surprise.

"No. Why? Should I have?" She didn't understand why he would ask. What was so special about the spare bedroom Damon had turned into an office?

"I thought Aspyn would have told you." His voice held a tone of disbelief. "Come on, let me show you."

His hard-soled work boots banged against the wood floor as he made his way to the office without bothering to look behind him to see if she followed. Down the hall the office door stood open. She'd passed it a few times, never bothering to look inside. Now she was curious. She couldn't help but follow the strong back of her tour guide, her gaze gliding lower to his jeans riding low on his hips.

Josh stood waiting by the door for her. Inside, she found her camera equipment. She hadn't bothered to ask Aspyn if it had arrived. She hadn't picked up a camera since her parents had died a month ago.

Everything was set up for her, waiting for her to get back to work. *They did this for me?*

"The door over there leads to the darkroom we put in for you. It was Aspyn's idea. I can't believe she didn't tell you." His wet curls dripped onto her shirt.

"Why didn't she say anything?"

"I don't know. Maybe she wanted it to be a surprise. I hope I didn't ruin it. We just finished it when you arrived." He reached for his cell on the desk next to one of her cameras.

"Could I borrow your phone? I want to call her. Mine's dead."

"Sure," he said, handing her his cell phone. "I'll wait in the living room to give you some privacy."

She stood there looking around the room, trying to take it all in. Aspyn did this for her. She still couldn't believe it.

She dialed Aspyn's number.

"No, it's Sarah."

Her friend asked why she had Josh's phone.

"He left it here by mistake and when he came back with for it, he let your surprise about the office slip."

Aspyn was silent on the other end.

"I hope he didn't spoil anything for you. He thought you would have told me. Why didn't you?" Sarah added when Aspyn remained silent.

Listening to her friend, she realized she was a little closed off since she'd pulled into the driveway. "I'm sorry. I didn't mean to be such a downer."

Aspyn tried to cut her off.

"That's no reason to act like that. You have changed your plans and opened your house for me. Look at what you did to make me feel at home and I was rude."

She listened to her friend explain why she did it, and it made her feel sadder. She told Aspyn when she was packing her cameras up to send them that she didn't know why she didn't just sell them, since she hadn't snapped a picture in over a month. Losing her parents in the way she did took her desire for photographs out of life. She left like a fish out of water. She didn't know what to do with her life, or her time.

"Aspyn, this means a lot to me. Thank you." She didn't know when or if she would pick up a camera again, but the meaning behind this meant the world to her. They were best friends, and Aspyn would make sure she got through this.

They talked for a little while longer and made plans for Sarah to go over for lunch the next afternoon. She hit the end button and took another look around the room, noticing her pictures of California, of her and Aspyn, and one with her with her parents.

Aspyn had put a lot of thought and work into making this room special for her. It was time to pull herself out of the grief that surrounded her and start living again. Her parents wouldn't want to see her this way. As for Cain, he didn't matter any longer. She needed to push him out of her thoughts.

Chapter Three

"Everything okay?" Sarah asked when she noticed Josh standing by the living room window, rubbing his temple.

"The tree Damon and I were going to take down beat us to the punch." He continued to stare out the window.

"What?" she asked, coming around the couch to stand next to him.

With the flash of lightening lighting up the sky, she could see an old oak tree had fallen across her driveway within inches of their vehicles, leaving it impossible to get in or out of the cabin's driveway.

"It was stuck by lightening in the last storm, but Damon thought it could wait until our youngest brother Mason gets home."

"Oh no!" she cried.

"I'll have to leave my truck here, but I can walk around the lake to Damon and Aspyn's house."

It was pouring rain; he would be soaked by the time he made it there. "I can't let you do that. Why don't you just stay here? You can have the bedroom. I'll sleep out here."

"Thank you. But I can't take your bedroom. I'll sleep on the couch, if you don't mind. It's what I would do at Damon's, anyway. They haven't decided on furniture for most of the house and there isn't any guest room furniture yet. Aspyn just broke down and bought the bedroom suite she loved, when they couldn't come to a decision together. It's one of the only rooms fully decorated."

"Seriously?"

"Yeah. Those two have a difference of option, but Damon is slowly realizing that it's better to make Aspyn happy than get his way. Plus, after the furniture is there, he sees she was right all along. He hated the bedroom suite she chose, complaining about it up until it was delivered and set up."

Sarah covered her mouth to stifle a giggle.

"Laugh all you want. I feel bad for Aspyn. My brother is hard to live with. She had no idea what she agreed to when she said yes to marriage."

That made her laugh more. "She loves him."

"Love. Remind her of that when she's ready to kick him in the ass, or when she's chasing the dozen kids he wants to have," he said, giving her a smirk.

"A dozen?" Her eyes must have been as big as saucers as she said that. She just couldn't believe a dozen.

"Close enough. I think last I heard, it was five or six. But still."

Knowing Aspyn as Sarah did, she was already on board with that number. "Seems they might be the perfect pair, after all." When Josh gave her a questioning look, she explained, "Aspyn loves kids, always wanted a bunch of her own."

He rolled his eyes and let out a puff.

"You don't like kids?" she asked, interested in his reaction to how many kids Aspyn and Damon wanted.

"I like kids, but I don't want that many. I'd like two or three. All girls."

"Girls? I thought men always wanted a son."

"Yeah. I want daddy's little girls. What about you?"

She'd thought about children a few times in the last couple of years, but Cain never thought it was the right time for marriage or kids. There was always an excuse. "Yeah, I want children."

Maybe I should consider single parenthood and get a sperm donor. Children have always been important to me, but do I want to do it alone? I wanted to give Mom and Dad grandchildren while they were alive. Now it's too late. If they were alive, I would be more comfortable doing the single parent thing. Dad would have been around to act like a father figure, teaching her son, if she had one, how to throw a football, fish and all the other things she couldn't teach him. But now there was no one. It was something she would have to give more thought to. Her parents' deaths made her reconsider everything.

"Sarah?"

"I'm sorry." She shook her head, pushing away the thoughts.

"You okay?"

"Yeah, sorry, I was just thinking. Did you say something?"

"Yeah, I asked you what made you move to this hick of a town from California."

"Oh. My parents passed away a few weeks ago, and everything changed for me. Aspyn seems so happy here, and she is my best friend." *Why did I really come here?* She couldn't honestly answer, but she wanted to be closer to Aspyn.

"It's going to be a big change from California." He plopped down on the couch.

"Oh I know." She chuckled. "I've already noticed that. It's so quiet here. I don't miss the police sirens, but without the traffic noise it seems dead here. How does anyone live without the noise?"

"You'll get used to not having the city noise. Trust me, there is nothing better than sitting on your porch in the cool, morning air with a hot cup of coffee, listening to the birds. The smell of the trees after a good rain, when everything is covered in the morning dew."

"You sound like you love it here."

"I wouldn't want to live anywhere else."

As Fate Would Have It

Chapter Four

After hours of talking, Sarah excused herself to get some sleep. Josh lay on the couch staring at the ceiling, thinking about her. *What is it about her that draws me in?* He had been anxiously waiting for Sarah to arrive. Something about the way Aspyn spoke of Sarah made part of him come alive. He wanted to get to know her. Wanted to know what type of person she was. What she loved, what made her tick and all the details in between.

She seems more upset than she is showing. Is it just the loss of her parents, or is there something more? His gut told him there was something more. Some deep hurt that came after her parents passed. Something that was making it hard for her to let go of the past.

His eyes drifted shut, and he let his guards fall, allowing him to sense what he was missing.

Could she let someone in? Or would she block him at every turn? He was going to do whatever it took to get to make Sarah his.

She's my mate.

* * *

Always an early riser no matter what time he went to sleep, Josh woke just after the sun rose. *I'll make her breakfast.* He stretched his arms above his head, working out the kinks from sleeping on the couch before heading to the kitchen.

He'd helped Aspyn with the groceries the day before. There was enough food for Sarah to hole up in here for weeks. Aspyn had bought all of her friend's favorites and more.

He grabbed the bacon. Once he got it sizzling on the stove, he turned his attention to the red pepper and onion. After dicing those, he got them cooking in another skillet. Once the bacon was done, he would crumble some of it up to add to the vegetables and make omelets.

He was enjoying a cup of coffee that had just finished perking while he was waiting for the omelets to finish. He sensed her moving toward the kitchen before he heard her bare feet on the wood floors.

"Morning." Sarah's voice was still full of sleep as she came around the corner, her grey lounge pants, and white tank top wrinkled from sleeping in them. "Something smells delicious."

"I hope I didn't wake you too early. To make up for crashing on your couch, I thought I would surprise you with breakfast."

"No. It's fine. Thank you. What are you making?"

He poured her a cup of coffee and handed it to her. He already had the creamer that Aspyn said she enjoyed setting on the table. "One of my favorite dishes. Omelets with red pepper, onion and bacon."

"Sounds wonderful," she said, pouring the cream into her coffee and bringing her cup close to her face as if to soak in the aroma.

"I hope you enjoy it. It's almost done." He forced his attention back to the stove, adding the cheese to the top of the omelet. Anything to take his mind off grabbing her and doing all of the naughty things that ran through his mind.

"I appreciate this, but you really didn't have to do it." She watched him, holding her coffee cup like it was a lifeline.

The cheese melted, and he placed the omelets on plates. "I know." He set the plate in front of her. "I hope you like it." He hoped making breakfast for her would allow him to get to know her better, but the real reason was to give him more time with her. He didn't want to leave her—he wanted to draw her into his arms.

"I'm sure I will." She set her coffee down and picked up the fork.

He sat across from her, watching her as she took a bite.

"This is delicious. Thank you."

"You're welcome." He smiled into the vibrant face of the woman who would be his mate before digging into his own breakfast.

Chapter Five

Two hours after breakfast, Aspyn and Sarah sat on the porch watching Damon and Josh cut down the tree. Sarah couldn't take her eyes off Josh. His toned, tanned muscles constricting as he worked drew her attention to his body. The way his jeans hugged his ass as he bent over had desire spreading through her. She couldn't remember the last time a man had turned her on as much as he did. She sure the hell had never felt anything like it through all her years with Cain. *Not that he did manual labor. No, that was beneath him.*

"Good–looking, isn't he?" Aspyn asked.

"What?" She looked away, unable to meet Aspyn's eyes, as her cheeks heated with embarrassment.

"Don't play me, girl. We have known each other too long, and I caught you watching him. You were practically drooling."

"I was not," she feverishly denied.

"So you admit you were watching," Aspyn said with a smile.

She was caught, and there was no use denying it. "Okay. So what if I was?"

"Good for you. Josh is almost as delicious as Damon."

"I don't need to get involved with anyone. Not right now."

Knowing her friend as well as she did, Aspyn was probably already plotting how to get them together. *This draw to him seems too soon. I just met him—I don't need this now.*

"Hey, I didn't say anything." Aspyn held up her hands as if to say she was innocent, but Sarah knew better.

"I think the four of us should have dinner tonight." Aspyn sipped her coffee, watching the men as they worked.

"See, I knew you were plotting something."

"Not plotting. Just a suggestion. Josh eats with us a few times a week. No use in him cooking for just himself when I always have leftovers. Same thing for you. You might as well come over and eat with us."

To Sarah that sounded like an excuse. But what could it hurt? Dinner with them would allow her to get to know Josh a little bit, yet still be able to maintain the distance she wanted. "I don't know."

"Oh come on." Aspyn turned to face Sarah. "You like him, and he's a good guy. What is the harm?"

"I'm not ready to get involved with anyone."

"You said that. I'm not asking you to get involved. I'm just inviting you for dinner. You need to eat—why shouldn't you eat with us?"

Aspyn had a point, but Sarah also knew there was a hidden agenda in there. Against her better judgment, she agreed. "Okay. But only tonight," she added, trying to make it clear to Aspyn that it was a one-time thing.

"We'll see," she heard Aspyn say under her breath as she turned back to watch the men.

Desperate to change the subject, she asked about Mason. "Josh mentioned a younger brother Mason and something about wanting to wait to cut the tree down until he was here. Where is he?"

"The rebel… He joined the Marines out of high school. He was shot in the shoulder and lost some mobility in his arm. He was honorably discharged and will return home soon."

"Why did you call him the rebel?" Sarah glanced toward Aspyn for a moment before letting her gaze wander back to the men.

She chuckled. "I haven't met him, but that's how Damon and Josh refer to him. Mason is stubborn, always bucking the system. Everyone was surprised he made in in the Marines. He left home to make his own path. They might nag him, but deep down they are both proud of him."

Sarah leaned back in her chair, soaking up the sun. Anyone observing her would have thought she was watching the men working, but her memories had her spiraling down a deep hole. A few years ago she was in the same spot with her parents as she watched Cain and some of their friends. Her parents had a large tree fall during an earthquake, and she'd asked Cain to help. *Boy was that a mistake.* Cain made her pay for it. *Looking at it now, I should have realized Cain was all about himself. He didn't care for anyone. Only doing things for himself, never bothering to think how it would affect someone else. Why did I never realize what he was?*

Aspyn touched her shoulder. "Sweetie."

"What?"

"You okay? You're crying?"

Sarah raised her hand, touching her cheek, and sure enough it was wet. She quickly wiped her eyes. "I'm fine."

"Are you sure?"

"I'm fine." Her voice turned nasty, making Aspyn move back. Shaking her head, she continued, "I'm sorry. I didn't mean that. I was just thinking."

"Do you want to talk about it?"

"No," she said, shaking her head. "It's nothing."

"It isn't nothing. Something has upset you," Aspyn said, wrapping her arm around Sarah.

"I was just thinking about my parents' tree that came down in the last earthquake."

"I don't understand."

"Cain and some of our friends helped cut up the tree. But…"

Aspyn interrupted her before she could continue. "Oh, I can only guess how well he took that."

She gave Aspyn a questioning look. "What? I thought you…you never spoke negatively about him."

"I never said a lot of things, but that didn't mean I liked him. He was a jerk. You deserved so much better."

Sarah rubbed her forehead, trying to digest what she was hearing. "Why now?"

"Maybe so you won't make the same mistake again. You deserve someone who will cherish you. Cain only valued himself."

She nodded, staring off into space. "I'm finally realizing it."

"It's about time, sweetie. I'm just sorry it happened the way it did."

She laid her head on Aspyn's shoulder. "Me too."

"Now you need to live for the moment. Like you told me when I moved here." Aspyn wrapped her arm tighter around Sarah.

Live for the moment. Sarah looked toward Josh as she wondered if she could include him in her living-for-the-moment plans. He dropped one of the logs they were cutting onto the wheelbarrow as their gazes met. Sparks flew between them, making her heart skip a beat.

Chapter Six

That night after dinner, Sarah was alone sitting on the porch wondering how she would adapt to the slower life here. *Could I really adjust to the slower pace? If I'm sticking around, maybe I should get a dog. Maybe a German Sheppard.*

Taking a long swig of her beer, she leaned her head back and closed her eyes. Another storm was brewing, bringing a cool evening breeze to dance around her. If she was honest with herself, she loved the peace and quiet of the area.

She must have dozed off. The next thing she heard was a truck door shutting, jarring her.

"I didn't mean to wake you." Josh stood by his truck in the driveway.

"I wasn't sleeping," she tried to lie, but her voice betrayed her.

"Sure," he mocked.

"What are you doing here?"

He opened the passenger door and reached in. "I thought you could use this."

On the passenger seat she could see a DVD player and a dozen or so movies. "You bought me a DVD player?"

"I knew you didn't have cable here yet and even if you call them on Monday, it's going to take a few days for them to come out. I figured by then you would be climbing the walls." He shot her a toe-curling smile before grabbing the items from the seat.

"Thank you. I believe Aspyn supplied the popcorn in her shopping trip. Why don't you join me for a movie, and I'll make the popcorn?"

"Extra butter and you got a deal."

"A man after my own heart." She held the door open for him. While he set the DVD player up, she headed over to the kitchen to make the popcorn. Before moving here, she'd sworn off men until she could get her life together, yet Josh made her throw that out the window. His laid-back attitude put her at ease, while drawing her into him.

"Movie's starting." Josh leaned against the doorframe.

She drizzled the melted butter across the bowl of popcorn before giving it a stir. "Perfect timing." She handed him the bowl and headed to the refrigerator. "Beer?"

"Sure."

She grabbed two beers and followed him back to the living room. Looking at the way his buns as she went…time to let her hair down and forget the troubles of her past—after all, that's what she came here to do. Move forward.

* * *

Setting the empty popcorn bowl aside, Josh knew it was time to make his move. He wrapped his arm around Sarah's shoulders, tracing his finger up and down the part of her arm he could reach. "How about having dinner with me tomorrow night?"

"Umm."

"Wait. Before you answer, hear me out. Sarah, you're an attractive woman, and I want to get to know you more. I feel as if I already know you through Aspyn. I know you went through some shit, which is why you wanted a change. I heard bits and pieces of it from Damon. But that doesn't mean you should stay holed-up in this cabin. Let me take you out and show you the town."

"I've got a lot of baggage." She nibbled on her lip.

"As do I, but that doesn't mean we don't deserve a chance at the same happiness that Damon and Aspyn have." He placed his hand over hers, giving it a light squeeze. "Sometimes that just means we have to fight harder for it."

"I don't know…"

"I won't push. You can think of it as a friendly evening out. I'll be your tour guide for the evening. What do you say?"

"Okay." She gave him a timid smile.

To get Sarah to open up to him, he would have to take it slow and not rush her, even while his animal demanded her. He wouldn't rush her.

Chapter Seven

Sarah stared into her closet, wondering what she would wear to dinner. She was more of a jeans and t-shirt kind of girl, so before moving here, she'd taken the dresses and other clothes she didn't wear to the thrift store. There was no use lugging them across the country only to have them hang in a closet.

It's been too long since I've been on a date. I've forgotten what it feels like. She put her hand on her stomach, trying to will the butterflies to calm.

She was debating about calling the whole thing off, when her cell rang. Plopping down on the bed, she reached for the phone. "Hello?"

Aspyn's voice filled the line, calming her nerves for a moment.

"Umm, no I can't come to dinner tonight. I'm going out with Josh." She held her breath, waiting for her friend's reaction.

Aspyn didn't let her down—the excitement in her voice almost washed away the fears Sarah had about the evening.

"I don't know if this was such a good idea…"

She was cut off by Aspyn's encouragement.

"I don't know. It's been years since I was on a date. You know Cain didn't fancy going out often. No, there is no need for you…" Before she could finish the sentence, the line was dead and Aspyn was on her way over.

She tossed the phone back onto the bed and stood. She had to have something that she could wear tonight. *If I knew where he was taking me, I'd have a better idea what to wear. Where can you even eat in a small town like this?*

"Sarah?" Aspyn called, shattering Sarah's thoughts.

"In the bedroom," she hollered back as the front door closed.

Moments later, Aspyn stood in the bedroom doorframe, her arms loaded with clothes, a couple pairs of shoes dangling from her fingertips.

"What is all that?"

"I know you. You needed something to wear. We don't have time to go shopping. Thankfully, we are the same size." Aspyn dropped the shoes to the floor before laying the clothes on the bed. "We might not have any fancy restaurants like we did in California, but you're not going out with Josh in jeans and a t-shirt."

She let out a heavy sigh. "Where is he taking me?"

"How should I know? You agreed to the date. I didn't set this up. If I know Josh, I suspect he will take you to Rizzo's. It's a family-owned Italian restaurant on the edge of town. It's quiet, romantic and they have delicious food. No matter what you order, you can't go wrong." Aspyn dug through the clothes she brought with her. "What about this?" She held up a white sundress with red swirls through it.

"You know I don't wear dresses often."

"I know, but tonight it's called for. Second date you can wear whatever you want. Tonight, however, is a different story. Josh and you are perfect for each other. He hates to get dressed up as well, but tonight he'll dress to impress you. You don't want to be underdressed."

She always cons me into doing what she wants. How does she do it? "Okay, but no heels." That was where Sarah planned to put her foot down.

"We'll see. What time is he picking you up?"

"Four." Sarah hung the dress on the back of the door.

"Four! Why so early? We only have an hour. You should have called me earlier."

Sarah couldn't help but chuckle at the horror on Aspyn's face. "He offered to show me around town before dinner. We need sunlight to see anything. We have plenty of time."

"Plenty of time. You're kidding me, right?"

Sarah leaned against the wall to keep from falling as her body shook with laughter.

"Don't stand there laughing. We have your hair and makeup to do before you can get dressed. Time is not on our side. Go plug in your curling iron. While that's heating, we will work on your makeup."

"We are not over-doing it," Sarah said, glaring at Aspyn. "It's bad enough I'm wearing a dress."

"I'm just going to add more curls to your hair, doing my best to bring out the natural wave before we sweep it up into a clip. I know you prefer your hair off your neck. Then we'll add a touch of makeup. That's all. I'm not going to make you look like a streetwalker. You should have more trust in me."

Sarah sat there while Aspyn fixed her makeup as if she was going to prom, and for the first time in months, hope filled her. Coming here put everything back on track for Sarah. Being close to Aspyn again gave her the sense that things would work out. She'd lost her family, but with Aspyn, Damon and Josh she was beginning to feel as if she belonged again. The small country town was quickly beginning to feel like home.

Chapter Eight

Josh had just put his truck in park when Aspyn came out of the house with her arms full. Jumping out of the truck, he rushed around to help her.

"What are you doing here?" he asked, holding open her car door.

"I was helping Sarah get ready. You better get in there before she decides to change her mind," Aspyn teased, tossing the extra outfits in the backseat before turning back around. "Friendly advice—she's my best friend and I love her like a sister. I haven't told her about our condition yet. I wanted to do that in person. I planned on telling her at the wedding, but then her parents passed and she moved here. The point is, she needs to know. Tell her before you steal her heart. If you wait, she'll see it as a betrayal, and you might lose her."

"You know that's a fine line there, Aspyn. Telling people what we are will only bring the hunters to our doorsteps. What if she can't handle the information?" He watched the house, wishing that his ability didn't always hang over his head like a dark cloud.

"She's stronger than most people think. She'll handle it. Tell her." With that, she got in the car and drove away, leaving Josh standing there.

Will she take it better knowing Aspyn has the same ability, or will she see it as deceit that she wasn't told before she moved across the country?

Sarah stepped onto the porch, the screen door slamming shut behind her. She stood there in a ray of sunshine, looking as if she just stepped out of a magazine cover. Her golden brown hair twisted up off her neck, leaving a few stray curls dangling, making him want to run his tongue down the side of her neck. The short sundress showed off her long legs, and the wedge sandals gave another inch of height to her body.

"Wow. You look incredible." He walked up the two steps to the cabin porch without taking his eyes off her. His muscles rolled smoothly, gliding him across the pavement to her.

"Are you sure? Maybe I should change?"

He grabbed hold of her arm before she could walk back inside. "No, you look beautiful. All eyes are going to be on you when we go to dinner." He leaned in to kiss her cheek.

"Only 'cause I'm the new girl in town."

"Heads might turn when someone new comes to town, but that won't be why they watch you tonight. The men won't be able to keep their eyes off you. I might have to fight them off." He gave her a big grin. "You ready?"

"Let me just grab my purse and cell."

A few moments later, they were ready and walking down the steps. As he pulled out his keys, it hit him. "Oh. I didn't think...?"

"What's wrong?" she asked, concern clear on her face.

"I should have borrowed someone's car. A truck is hard to get in and out of in a dress. Would you like to take your car?"

"No. It's fine. I love trucks. It wasn't practical in California for a truck, at least not for me, or I would have had one. I always feel like an ant in the car with all the big trucks and SUV's driving past." She laughed.

She has a beautiful laugh, and that smile could be the death of me.

"Are you sure?" He hit the unlock button, and the truck's lights flashed.

"I'm sure." He opened her door, watching as she skillfully maneuvered herself in. To his disappointment, she managed to do it without flashing him.

* * *

The drive around town was beautiful. He showed her where the small shopping plaza that held the grocery store was before heading into the quiet town. Main Street was full of quaint little shops, giving the town a homely feel. She saw kids playing in the streets, mothers pushing strollers, someone out walking their dog. It was a small town where everyone seemed to know everyone, a place she always hoped to one day settle down.

"Auntie Jane's?" she asked as she watched a woman change the sign in the window to closed.

"It's a bakery. You'll have to try Auntie Jane's. She has a talent other people wish they could compete with. I'm surprised the town doesn't waddle. Most of the residents stop in a few times a week."

"Perfect. I have a sweet tooth. It's great there is a nearby bakery to satisfy it. Hopefully when I leave here, my clothes will still fit," she joked, looking out the window.

"Aspyn said you might not stay here. What are your plans?"

"I don't know. Aspyn is all I have left, since my parents died a little over a month ago. I always believed I would settle down in a quiet town. The city is ingrained in me, but I'm not sure it works for me any longer. I promised Aspyn that I would stay until after the wedding to help her. So I'm here for the next few months at least.

Maybe I'll fall in love with the area and won't want to leave."

"Maybe you'll find someone worth sticking around for." He put his hand on her leg.

She tensed. "I'm not looking for someone. Love suits Aspyn, but it isn't part of my destiny."

"How can you say that? You see what Aspyn and Damon have. How can you not want that for yourself?"

"I'm a realistic. Love is unrealistic. It deceives you." She stared out the window.

"Sarah, I realize you have been hurt, but that is no reason to give up finding your mate…your true love. You have to open yourself to it and allow it in when you find it. You will have the love that Aspyn has."

Silence filled the truck as they drove toward the restaurant. Forcing love and relationships on Sarah was a quick was to end an evening, and he didn't want that. He'd change the subject now, but he wouldn't let Sarah deny him as her mate. They deserved love, and he would see they had it.

"What about work?"

"I do freelance graphic design work. There are a few companies I do a lot of promotional material for. It allows me to make my own hours, as long as I meet the deadlines, and to work wherever I want. I'm hoping the cable company can come install my Internet before the end of the week. I have a large project due next week. I used to do a little photography on the side as well, but that was more as a hobby then actual work."

"I'd offer you the use of my Internet anytime you would like, but it's a bit of a drive. I leave in the next county over where my construction company is based. It's about a fifteen to twenty minute drive. However, the offer stands if you'd like. I'm not home during the day, so you'd have the place to yourself and could work without being disturbed." He turned the truck off Main Street, coming to a busier road.

It would be a perfect opportunity to pop home and spend my lunch hour with her, without being too overbearing. Maybe get her to stay the night with my arms wrapped around her.

"Thank you. Aspyn offered as well, but I told her no. It's hard to work with her there. I know she is still trying to get the house organized, and she doesn't need me hanging out for hours at a time. I'm sure they'll be able to get it installed soon. I'll call on Monday."

"Just let me know." He tried to hide his disappointment as he turned into Rizzo's restaurant.

Chapter Nine

"Dinner was amazing. Thank you," she said as they pulled into her driveway.

"You're welcome. Rizzo's is one of the best places around. You couldn't go into the city and get a better meal."

The truck came to a halt in front of the porch. "It's still early yet. Would you like to come in for a beer?"

"Sure. I wanted to talk to you about something, anyway." He jumped out of the truck and walked around to open her door.

What a gentleman! I don't think anyone ever opened a door for me before.

Taking his outreached hand, she stepped out of the truck. "Have a seat on the porch. I'll grab the beers." Before she could move away from him, he lowered his head and kissed her gently on the lips. It was over as quickly as it started, giving her a brief glimpse into what could be in store for the future.

Out of the corner of her eye, she saw something scurry past the other side of the pond. *What was that?* It was too large to be a dog. Being on four legs, it ruled out a human. She paused on the second step, watching to see if she saw it again. *I could have sworn it was…* She shook her head. *No, that's impossible.*

Slowly turning her head to look at Josh, she found him staring at the pond. "Did you see that?"

"It was nothing. All kinds of animals live in the woods."

She was horrified to think of large animals so close to her cabin. *What if they attack?* Stepping toward her, he placed a hand on her arm. "Don't worry. They won't hurt you."

Inside, she wasn't sure about that. She'd heard horror stories of wild animals attacking. While packing her apartment in California, she heard on the news a mountain lion attacked a man on a walking trial. He almost died. There are no mountain lions, she calmly tried to tell herself, but it didn't calm her nerves.

"I'll get the beers." She took one last look toward the pond before opening the cabin door. It was a cool summer evening, and the breeze would air out the cabin. While sliding open the living room windows, her gaze wondered to the pond again. She couldn't shake the feeling that something was amiss. Slipping her feet out of the wedge shoes, she padded barefoot to the kitchen.

Snatching two beer bottles from the refrigerator, she hurried back to the porch. She left the front door open to allow the breeze in and let the screen slam shut behind her. Josh leaned against the porch railing, staring down at his feet.

"Here you go." She held out a beer for him.

"Thanks." He twisted off the cap, setting it on the railing.

Something had changed in the last few minutes, and she couldn't put her finger on it. Throughout their date, there was never an awkward silence. They got along as if they had known each other for ages. He'd learned more about her over a short dinner then Cain had known in all the years they were together. Just another reminder that he never really cared for her. But now Josh fiddled with the change in his pocket, looking uncomfortable.

"Is something wrong, Josh?" The click of coins hitting together filled the heavy silence. With the silence lingering as an unwelcome guest, she became tense. Minute after minute ticked by as Josh remained quiet. Plucking the courage, she took a deep breath. "I had a wonderful time tonight, but you don't have to stay if you have somewhere to be."

"Sarah, you are an amazing woman. I enjoyed tonight with you…"

"Oh. I know where this is going." She took a long swing from her beer.

"I don't think you do. Please let me finish." When she nodded, he continued. "I'm concerned that what I have to tell you will make you end what could happen between us before it even begins."

"Then why say it?"

He smiled halfheartedly. "If I don't tell you, Aspyn will. I'm taking her advice and being up front with you about it."

"Let's get it over with. What is it?" She set her beer aside.

"What you saw tonight…was a mountain lion shifter."

She cut him off with a deep laugh. "Shifter, huh?" she said between laughs.

"Yes. It was a person who could change into an animal. In this case, a mountain lion." He placed his untouched beer next to the cap on the railing. "I know this because I can do the same thing."

This was mind-boggling. She blinked at him and for a brief second wondered if he had been replaced by aliens or something. This didn't seem like the same man she'd spent the last few hours with laughing and having a good time.

"You're delusional." She grabbed her beer. "I think you should leave now."

"Sarah, please let me finish."

"There is nothing more to say. It is obvious that you are making this up so I don't want to see you again. Or to scare me away. Well, you succeeded. I promised Aspyn I'd stay until her wedding but once it's over, I'm leaving. I know you're the best man and it is unavoidable we will see each other in the meantime, but please keep your distance."

"Sarah, please." She slammed the screen door shut, only seconds later to be followed by the main door.

"I should have never listened to Aspyn. I told her it was too soon to tell you. Give you time to settle was my suggestion, but she told me it would only make you resent me for not telling you sooner," she heard him say through the front porch window before he stormed off the porch.

Chapter Ten

It wasn't until she heard his truck peel out of the driveway, tossing up loose stones on the way, that was she able to relax. She slid down the back of the door, cradling her head, as the tears fell.

Aspyn knew, and she didn't tell me? Better yet, why would she push us together if he's delusional? She was half tempted to call Aspyn, but she wasn't in the mood to hear whatever excuse her friend would come up with.

Frozen, she wondered if coming here wasn't a big mistake. Leaving behind everything she knew, starting over again, and getting far away from Cain seemed like the best solution. She was tired of Cain's stunts, especially this last one.

Showing at her parents' funeral drunk, then making a scene when she wouldn't leave to take him to a party they planned to attend. She never understood how he could have expected her to leave the funeral services to attend a party. Her parents lay in caskets, and all he could think about was himself. Still, she might have forgiven him for that if it wasn't for what came after.

Her ringing cell phone brought her back to the present and chased the depressing memories away. Unfolding her body, she stood, making her way to the table where she tossed her purse. She grabbed her phone.

Aspyn calling.

Anger made her blood run hot as she read the display. *Not now.* She hit the ignore button and dropped the phone back in her purse. She wasn't ready to deal with Aspyn, not when her hurt feelings were so close to the surface. She expected better from her friend. The betrayal ran deep— first Cain now Aspyn, leaving her alone in this world.

* * *

Josh found Damon and Apsyn sprawled out in their mountain lion forms on the deck. No one came around these parts much. If anyone did, the three of them could smell the person before they arrived, giving them plenty of time to shift and dress.

They knew he was there and could smell his anger, but they laid there enjoying the last of the sun as it sank low in the sky.

"Aspyn, you didn't tell her that you're a shifter? Why didn't you tell me she knew nothing? I thought she knew about you. This is entirely your fault. You pushed me to tell her, I did and she kicks me out. Get dressed," Josh, growled coming to stand at the deck.

His animal wanted to shift, to run through the woods and feel the cool summer air in his hair, but he had to deal with Aspyn first. He had to find a way to win Sarah over.

It was finally sinking in. All those years of searching for his mate, and he'd finally found her, only to be cast aside. *Mated?* He couldn't believe it.

For years, he searched for his mate, wanting to settle down and start a family. His business took off quickly, allowing him the stability he wanted before starting a family. Everything fell into place, except finding a mate.

He stood on the porch staring across the pond at Sarah's cabin. *What was she doing? Probably packing.* Just the thought of her packing tore his heart.

Damon returned with a pair of khaki shorts on and two beers in hand. "What the hell happened?"

"Where's Aspyn? I only want to go through it once."

"She's trying to call Sarah. What happened?" Damon took a swig of his beer before lowering himself onto one of the porch chairs.

"Everything was going fine until we arrived back at the cabin. She was going into the house when she saw you and Aspyn out for your evening run." He glared at Damon. "It seemed the best time as any to tell her."

The screen door creaked open as Aspyn came out of the house. "She didn't answer. The call went to voicemail. What happened once you told her?"

"She said I was delusional and told me to leave. She slammed the door in my face before I could explain. This is your fault, Aspyn. You said she could handle it and I should tell her. Well, she isn't handling it very well. After your wedding, she's leaving. She wants nothing more to do with me." He stood pacing the deck. "Damn it, she's my mate."

Chapter Eleven

"Sarah, open this door!" Aspyn hollered from the porch.

Coward? Yeah, that's me. Sarah hid in the kitchen, unwilling to face Aspyn. She didn't know what she would say when she finally faced Aspyn. Part of her wanted to yell and scream at her friend for setting up the date, while the other part wanted to cry the loss of whatever could have developed with Josh. Her emotions were playing havoc with her.

"I know you're in there. I'm not leaving until I talk to you. Sarah, this is childish. Open up."

She heard Aspyn's footsteps moving across the porch. *Is she leaving?* Her hopes crashed when she heard the rocker creak.

Shit. She isn't going to leave.

Fifteen minutes passed and still Aspyn say on the porch, rocking gently. *Let's get this over with.* Sarah opened the door and stepped out on the porch.

"It took you long enough." Aspyn looked toward her. "Sit, we need to talk."

"I'm not really in the mood for this right now. I came out to ask you to go home. I feel awful that you're just sitting out here." She crossed her arms over her chest and stood close to the door.

"I'm not leaving until we talk. I don't care if I have to sit here all night. So why don't you just sit down and let's get it over with?"

"Fine." She plopped into the empty chair. "What do you want?"

"I want to talk to you about what happened between Josh and you last night."

"There is nothing to say. We had a nice dinner, but we won't be seeing each other again." She didn't want to discuss what happened. If Josh *was* delusional then what he said about Aspyn knowing this wouldn't have been true. At least that was what Sarah hoped.

"Don't give me that bull crap. Josh came over after he left last night and told us what happened. I know he told you that he is a mountain lion."

"So you did know?" Her heart skipped a beat. *Aspyn knew and yet still pushed us together? Why didn't she tell me?*

"I knew because I'm one." She lowered to the ground. Short, tawny hair started to form all over her body. Her

93

clothes ripped and fell to the floor as her body started to change and morph.

"What the hell?" Sarah squealed as she squirmed away from the large mountain lion that now stood on her porch. *This can't be happening. I'm not seeing this!*

She closed her hand around the door handle as Aspyn shifted back.

"We're not lying to you." Aspyn stood naked on two legs.

"This can't be happening. All the years we lived together, and you never told me." She held onto the doorframe, willing her legs to quit shaking.

"I didn't know about it." She reached to the side of the chair and pulled out a thin, cotton dress from her purse. She slipped it over her head before continuing. "It wasn't until I met Damon that I found out. I wanted to tell you. You called shortly after I found out. I told you he had some crazy stories, but wouldn't tell you what. Remember? I planned to tell you when I got back. I didn't come back, and it didn't seem like the best thing to tell you over the phone."

"You should have told me before I moved here." Sarah's legs threatened to go out from under her if she moved.

"Maybe I should have. But would you have believed me if I told you on the phone?" Aspyn's dress fell into place before she sank onto the rocker again.

"I guess not. I saw it happen, and I still don't believe it."

"See, it was something that had to be done in person. Then once you were here, the timing didn't seem right. I shouldn't have left it to Josh to tell you. Maybe it was the coward's way out, but it seemed appropriate to come from your mate. It's how I found out."

The world began to spin as her breath caught in her throat. "My what? Mate?"

Chapter Twelve

Mate? What did she mean by mate? For the last week, Sarah had been asking herself that very question. She sat in front of her computer trying to finish the website design that was due soon. The cable company couldn't come until the middle of the following week, leaving her only option to drive twenty minutes to the café in the next town, or the library. She preferred the café for the coffee and background noise.

The cell phone that lay next to the laptop caught her eye. How many times over the last week had she picked it up to call Josh only to put it down again? Her need to see him had become almost like an obsession. She craved him.

"I didn't realize how much I depended on the Internet until now," she whined to the empty room. "Another trip to the café tomorrow, and maybe I'll be able to finish it."

A knock on the door drew her attention away from the laptop. Setting it on the coffee table, she unfolded her body. *Who could that be? Aspyn and Damon had plans tonight, so it can't be them.*

She opened the front door to find Josh standing there. "Ah…what…umm," she stuttered.

"I had to see you. I didn't like how we left things last week. I need to explain, to make you understand." He stood with his hands in his pockets, jingling his keys as if he was uncomfortable.

"There's nothing to say." Her breath caught in her throat. It had been the longest week of her life. She was still having a hard time dealing with the fact he wasn't completely human, yet she couldn't help but hope to catch a glimpse of him or that he would stop by. Now here he stood on her doorstep, and she acted rude.

"On the contrary, I believe there is a lot to say."

"Fine." She moved aside. "Come in."

Inside she sat down on the couch, pulling her legs under her body, glaring at him.

"Did I interrupt your work?" He nodded toward the laptop.

"It's nothing. I can't do much without Internet. Tomorrow, I'll go to this little café I found and hopefully finish it."

"Sarah, I know you don't believe what I said the last time I saw you." He paced the small living room as he spoke.

"I didn't believe you then, but the truth has been brought to my attention." She let out a deep sign before continuing. "Aspyn showed up and shifted right there in front of me. Hearing it is still hard to believe but when you see it with your own eyes, you can't deny it."

Josh let out a deep laugh that had his eyes lighting up with amusement. She wasn't sure what he found funny, but she loved his laugh. It made her smile as she raised an eyebrow in question. "Sorry, it's just so like Damon to do something like that. Aspyn must be picking up his bad ways."

"Damon did that to convince her he wasn't crazy. She figured it was the only way to make me believe as well." Her lips curled into a smile as she watched him. "It worked, but it was an unpleasant surprise."

"Aspyn should have been the one to tell you. She should have told you before you came." He ran his hand through his curly black hair. "I didn't realize she didn't at least tell you about herself until I tried to tell you. You're her best friend, damn it. She should have told you."

"You're right, she should have. She knows she should have. Still it doesn't change the fact she didn't. She took the chicken's why out by making you tell me. There is something you can tell me, though." She bit her lip, unsure if she wanted to ask. The answer might be more than she wanted to handle.

"Anything." He lowered himself to sit next to her on the couch. "What's on your mind, sugar?"

"Sugar, huh?"

His lips curled into a smile, making her to want to kiss him. "It fits you. Your kisses are like sugar, making me want more of them. Maybe as payment for this question, you'll give me a kiss."

She rolled her eyes, laughing. "We'll see. Depends on the answer. Aspyn said she didn't tell me about shifters because it seemed appropriate to come from my mate. What did she mean by mate?"

"She never keeps her mouth shut, does she? Leave it to Damon to mate with someone who can't keep quiet." He shot up from the couch as if it had caught fire. Pacing the small living room, he ran his hand through his hair again. She was beginning to realize it was something he did when he was nervous.

"She does have foot-in-mouth disease. There you go using the *mate* word again. What does that mean?"

"Shifters have a true mate. Only once we have found our mate is sex enjoyable, and our mate is the only one we can have children with." He stood across the room, braced for her reaction.

"You can't have sex until you find a mate? What if you never find the person?"

"We can have sex—it's just not as enjoyable. It's more difficult. However, once we're mated, we can't be with another. Our bodies do not arouse by another's affections once we have mated. Shifters believe in fate. Fate will bring the mates together when the timing is right."

Does that mean now that he has found me—his supposed mate—that he can't be with anyone else? She took a few calming breaths and asked him. "Does that mean…you can't be…?"

"With anyone else?" he finished her question. "Yes, now that I have found you."

"Shouldn't your mate be a shifter like you? How do you know when you find your mate?" The questions ran from her as if she was a faucet.

"Not all mates are shifters. We can mate with humans, or even other shifter breeds. Women who are shifters can't shift until they find their mate; they need the mate to guide them through the process and almost always mate with a shifter." He sank next her to her again, wrapping her hand in his. "Shifters recognize their mates by the glow around them. It can only be seen by your mate. There's also a connection between us, pulling us together. You must feel it. It's almost as if we are magnets trying to connect to each other."

"I feel drawn to you, sure, but…" Her words were cut off as his lips covered hers. Devouring the willpower she had left to hold him off. She gave into his kiss. He cupped the back of her head, drawing them closer.

When they drew apart, her breath and fight were gone, replaced with desire.

Chapter Thirteen

"I need you," she whispered, their lips just inches apart.

Finally! He slid his arm behind her back and one under her legs, scooping her up. "It's wonderful to hear that." He kissed her forehead as she snuggled against his body.

"I can walk, you know."

"I know, but I want to carry you. We'll make it to bed quicker this way."

In the bedroom, he lowered her gently to sit on the edge of the bed before pulling her white tank top over her head. Their lips met again in a fury while he reached behind her to unhook her bra.

He tossed the bra to the bottom of the bed, moving his mouth down her neck to her perky nipples that were calling to him. Wrapping his lips around one of her nipples, drawing it into his mouth, he circled it with his tongue while he unbuttoned her jeans.

With his lips locked onto her nipple with tantalizing possessiveness, she tugged his t-shirt up his chest, running her fingers over his abs.

He let her nipple slide from his mouth as he pushed her down on the bed. She held onto his shirt and lay down, leaving him no choice but to slip it off. He tugged her jeans and panties down her legs, letting them pool at her bare feet. "Sugar, you're beautiful."

He wanted to take his time, making each moment special. He caressed every curve of her body, kissed his way up. When their lips met, the burning passion crackled through their bodies. He explored her mouth with a hunger that wouldn't be denied.

Standing, he slipped out of his jeans and boxers before perching himself on top of her. He placed his hands gently on her knees, spreading them, giving him the access that he desired. She moaned with expectation as his erection met her tender flesh.

He bit the inside of his cheek, forcing himself to ask, "You're sure? This will change our lives forever. Our mating will be complete. There will be no running from me."

"I'm sure. Please, Josh." Her voice was husky with unspent desire.

He nodded, slowly sliding his shaft into her wet core.

Around them the air sizzled as his shaft slid in her, his body covering her as he worked his way in and out.

As they found the tempo that bound their bodies together, passion throbbed through them, demanding to be released. Waves of ecstasy flooded through them. Her body squirmed beneath him as she neared her climax. Her fingers digging into his chest, she arched her back.

Ecstasy filled him to a breaking point; he threw his head back and roared. He slammed home one final time, making them both cry out with release.

He slid off her to lie next to her, her body cuddled close while they laid there in afterglow. She draped her leg over his and ran her hand over his chest as they held each other close.

* * *

She snuggled in his arms, running her fingers over his abs, his sun-drenched body called to her again.

What was I thinking? A shifter? How am I supposed to ever have the family I wanted?

"You look lost in thought, sugar. What's on your mind?"

She tried to smile at him, to tell him nothing, but her willpower was gone. "I'm thinking about my future. Maybe this was a mistake."

"I told you before—there's no turning back. You're my mate. Fate brought us together. How could that be a mistake?" He angled his body to look at her, gliding his forefinger across her jawline.

"I came here thinking of single parenthood. Adoption. Sperm donor. I was planning to make an appointment at the sperm bank, to discuss their services. It's time I made my dreams come true. I wanted a family, and I'm finally ready to make that happen. Now you show up. The timing is bad. I don't want to put my dream on hold any longer for a man, and I wouldn't expect you to hang around if I'm having another man's baby." She spit it out without pausing. She knew if she paused, he'd just interrupt her.

"So marry me. Let's have a family of our own." He said it as if it was the obvious solution.

"Be serious. We just met."

"Sugar, you're my mate. I've waited my whole life for you. For years I've looked for you, wanted to find my mate and have my own family."

Chapter Fourteen

Weeks later, summer turned to fall as the leaves started to change color and flutter rom the trees. On one of the last warm evenings, Sarah and Aspyn gathered on the porch, discussing her upcoming wedding.

"It's everything you want. Why won't you marry him?" Aspyn asked, flipping through the binder of wedding invitations she could choose from.

"It seemed too soon when he asked before. I was with Cain for years, and I still didn't know the true Cain. But I decided next time Josh asks me, I'll say yes. I love him."

"Cain was an asshole. Josh is not like that. You have to realize that by now." Aspyn turned the book to face Sarah. "What do you think of these?" The invitation was a creamy white with black swirls and raised gold lettering.

She has a point. Josh is nothing like Cain. I know I'm head over heels in love with him, but I know how quick things can change. Nausea hit her like a speeding freight train, making her lose her breath.

"Sarah, you okay?"

"I'm…" Words were caught in her throat as another wave of nausea hit her. "I'm not feeling very well all of a sudden."

"Maybe you should go lay down for a bit. Josh and Damon are working late to complete that house on time, but I can call Josh if you want him." Aspyn set the invitation book aside, her attention now directed at Sarah.

"No. I'm fine. Maybe I'll just lie down. I wasn't feeling well this morning, but then it passed." Sarah stood, ready to go inside.

"Sarah, could you be pregnant?"

Pregnant? Could I be pregnant? Sarah wanted to be pregnant, especially pregnant with Josh's child. They weren't taking any precautions, yet they weren't actively trying either.

* * *

The next morning, Aspyn's word still rang in Sarah's head. *Pregnant?* Why was something she wanted for so long make her all of the sudden petrified?

Four minutes until I know. The home pregnancy test lay on the bathroom counter. She'd followed the directions to the letter. Now only the time stood in her way. *Why can't time hurry?*

Her stomach did flip-flops as she passed the minutes by reading the directions again. One line—not pregnant. Two lines—pregnant.

* * *

Josh had found out his mate was ill just a few hours ago. He stopped by work to hand work off to his site manager and stopped by the supermarket for ginger ale and soup before rushing to Sarah's side.

Opening the cabin door, he found Sarah on the couch, her knees pulled tightly against her chest, rocking back and forth. Coming around the couch, he saw that tears ran down her face. "Sugar, what is it? Are you that sick? Should I take you to the hospital?"

She used the back of her hand to wipe her face. "No, I'm fine."

"Then why are you crying?" He pressed his hand against her forehead. *She doesn't feel hot.*

She shot from the couch and stalked toward the window. "I'm pregnant," she whispered, staring out the window.

His shifter hearing allowed him to hear her. "That's wonderful, sugar. That's what we wanted."

"We?" She hugged her stomach.

"Yes, we. I told you from the beginning that I wanted to marry you and start a family." He went to stand next to her. "I love you, Sarah. Will you marry me now?"

"I told Aspyn yesterday that the next time you asked, I'd marry you."

"Does that mean yes?"

"Yes. I love you Josh."

"But what about the child? Will he or she be like you?"

"Yes. If we have a son, he will go through the change around the age of ten, but our daughter's change will happen once she has found her mate. There is nothing to worry about. Our children will be surrounded by shifters and will be well supported through their transitions."

She nodded, as she already expected at least part of the answer. When she lay with him, she knew the chances of her becoming pregnant with a shifter child was possible.

She lived through the bad for a reason—Fate had given her everything she wanted in one move. Taking her from a lonely and heartbroken woman to a fiancée and an expectant mother in a very short time.

Mason's Fate

Chapter One

Mason Andrews stepped out of the taxi in from of his
brother, Damon's house, taking in his surroundings. The
red, yellow and gold leaves cluttered the ground, leaving no
doubt that fall was coming to an end. The first snowfall
wouldn't be long now, bringing the blast of winter to the
sleepy town.

It's good to be home. I didn't realize how much I missed it. He
rubbed his injured shoulder. They might have removed the
bullet, but it still pained him. Doctors said he'd never
regain complete mobility in his arm, leaving the Marines no
choice but to honorably discharge him. It was only a
month since the accident and already he missed the
adrenaline and action the Marines brought him.

The doctors were wrong. They weren't aware of his
healing ability. As a mountain lion shifter, wounds that
would be life-threatening to a human would heal. Still it

would take time, and once the healing was complete he had no way of explaining it to his commanding officers. It would bring up questions he was unable to answer. He wouldn't expose his people just to maintain his career.

The military was all he'd known since graduating high school, so adjusting wouldn't be easy. With determination, he grabbed his olive green military duffle bag, ready to face his brother.

Before he made it to the porch, the front door swung open, and a woman stepped out. She wore a loose cream sweater over black leggings, and her long brown hair hung free on her shoulders.

"Mason? Is that you? Damon and Josh were going to pick you up at the airport tonight."

He nodded. "You must be Aspyn. I caught an earlier flight. I told them before I'd get a taxi, but they didn't listen. Since I was early, I did just that. No use waiting around the airport for them. Is Damon home?"

"Come in. Sarah's inside. Damon and Josh are meeting with a potential client in town but should be back shortly."

He couldn't leave the woman standing in the cold even if he'd prefer to wait for Damon on the porch. Surrounded by women wasn't how he wanted to spend the afternoon.

"Come on, Mason. We don't bite. After all, in just two weeks' time we'll be family."

The reminder of that made his blood run cold. In two weeks there was to be a double wedding for Damon and Aspyn and Josh and Sarah, with him as the best man. The women said there was no reason to gather the family twice, and from what he heard, his brothers fell in line with what they wanted. He had a feeling if they asked for the moon, his brothers would do their best to see they got it.

Aspyn had the date set and was in the process of making arrangements when Sarah agreed to marry Josh. Minor changes allowed both women to have the wedding of their dreams, or so he was told.

Inside he found Sarah, clinging to a glass as if it were her lifeline. She sat bent over, her chest touching her knees and her face pale. "Mason, your other future sister-in-law Sarah."

"It's a pleasure to meet you finally. Josh talks highly of you. Please forgive my appearance…." She set the glass aside and ran from the room.

"Is she okay?" Mason tossed his duffle bag aside.

"Forgive her. It's morning sickness. Have a seat. I'm going to text Damon to let the guys know you arrived. Can I get you something to drink?" Aspyn grabbed her cell phone from the coffee table.

"No thanks." Taking in the room, he was in awe of the work Damon did to make this place beautiful. From the hand-carved railing on the stairs in the entryway, to the woodwork around the fireplace, everything had such detail. In the years he was away, Damon had become a talent to reckon with.

* * *

"Hey, bro. I hope our women didn't bore you with wedding details or try to scare you off children with their pregnancy pains." Damon stormed into the room, tossing his jacket on the back of the couch.

"No." He smiled for the first time since the accident. It was surprising how easy it was around his brothers. They lifted his spirits in a way nothing else could, without even trying. "Aspyn got an emergency call from the caterer and went into your office a little bit ago, and poor Sarah's spent more time in the bathroom than with me. Are you sure she is all right? Maybe Josh should take her to the hospital. I offered, but she told me it was part of being pregnant."

"She's fine. The doc says it will only last the first trimester. Josh went to check on her."

"If it's so normal, why isn't Aspyn dealing with it? Man, why didn't you tell me she was expecting too?"

"Different women, different pregnancy symptoms. I didn't tell you because she wanted to keep it hush. Aspyn was concerned how Sarah would handle it, but the worries were eliminated when Sarah got pregnant too."

"What?" He knotted his eyebrows together in confusion. "Why would she worry about that? Women get pregnant all the time."

Damon dropped into the chair, remote in hand, flicking on sports news as Josh wandered into the room.

"Sarah's world got turned upside down before moving here. Her parents died, she broke up with her boyfriend of many years— it was a bad time. She was considering single parenthood with a sperm donor when Josh came along."

"I'd appreciate it if you didn't mention it. She's finally settling down, and Aspyn says returning to her old self. Well when she isn't…." Josh raised his eyebrows, tilting his head toward the bathroom.

"I hardly think it will come up, Josh," he ragged his brother. "I go away for a little while and you both not only get engaged but you knock the women up. Talk about smooth movers. Gram would say that should have waited until the wedding night."

"Yeah, that old woman is probably rolling in her grave. She'd have busted our chops for it. But it's a different time than when Gram was raised." Josh sank into the corner of the sectional sofa on the opposite end of where Mason sat. "Enough about us. What are you going to do now that you're out of the Marines?

The dreaded question. What now? He had been asking himself that same question since the accident. *I'm a Marine. That's what I'm. I don't know how to do anything else.* His whole life revolved around the Marines. Two weeks after he graduated from high school, he was on the bus to boot camp, rarely returning home except once or twice a year on leave.

The minutes ticked by as he worked on an answer. To come up with an answer now, when he had been pondering it for weeks, was as likely as asking for rain on a cloudless day.

"I'm unsure. Coming back to civilian life was unexpected. I'll get a room at Daisy's Inn, until I find a place of my own." Unable to meet their gazes, he stared out the sliding glass door. He didn't want their sympathy— all he wanted things to be the way they were. A gust of wind blew more leaves from the branches, bringing home fast that things would never be the same. Life moved on, just as the seasons changed. There was no use living in the past. As the trees braced for winter, he must do the same and face the challenges that were in store for him.

Chapter Two

Damon insisted on Mason staying at the cabin Aspyn inherited from her father. There was no use staying at a hotel when the cabin was empty, his brother told him. It eliminated one problem–being around people–but made him just a stone's throw away from his family.

Damon and Aspyn just across the pond, and Josh and Sarah would soon be moving into the area. Josh had his crew working long hours to build Sarah's dream home. The construction site for it sat just between Damon's house and the cabin.

It all made him want to find a place of his own quickly. A quite little house in the middle of nowhere. Somewhere he could be alone and have the freedom to shift whenever he wanted. Sure here he could shift to his mountain lion form whenever he pleased, but he wouldn't be alone. Not with Damon and Josh living so close.

To take the chill out of the air he turned on the heat
before looking around the cabin. Sarah apologized that her
photography equipment and summer clothing still cluttered
the guest room. They saw no sense in moving things she
didn't need to Josh's current house, when they'd have to
lug it all back again in a few months. Not that the stuff
bothered him—he had no need for the second bedroom.
Besides checking the room to ensure there were no boxes
over the heating vents, he didn't disturb the possessions.

The main bedroom was done in warm tones. The
walls were a warm brown color, while the brown comforter
had white swirls that lightened the room. The large bay
window took advantage of the view of the pond, while the
heavy curtains tied back to the sides and allowed him to
close out the sun. The private en suite bathroom had the
same feel, but someone had added a touch of a pale blue in
the form of hand towels.

He tossed his military duffle bag next to the dresser,
not ready to unpack. The bag contained everything his old
life represented. His dress uniform, BUDs, and worst of all
the commendation for his bravery. The memory of the
incident was all too clear to him, and that commendation
only served as another reminder he didn't need.

He would have to deal with unpacking at some point,
but tonight he wanted to forget it and take in his
surroundings. Shifting would help relieve the tension that

tightened each of his muscles, but he didn't want relief. A walk was what he needed.

* * *

"Of all the times!" Tiffany Tyler kicked the front tire of her SUV. She was exhausted after spending the last eight hours in the car with her three-month-old daughter. The trip should have only taken a little over three hours, but Paige wanted held. Her darling baby girl was under the weather, making the trip almost impossible. *Why did I ever think traveling with Paige would be easy? I should have let Natalie come along.* At least then someone could have helped with the baby. Alone, she had to stop anytime her daughter cried.

Thirty miles ago, her vehicle started acting up. She begged and pleaded for it to get her home. Her luck only held until fifteen minutes ago. *Ten miles.* Kicking the tire again, she ran through her options. There was no way she could walk the ten miles with Paige.

She prayed for service as she slipped her cell phone out of her jeans pocket again. *No such luck.* Paige slept on in her car seat, but that wouldn't last long. The car would get cold soon and neither of them would last long in this weather. When they'd set out on the trip, it was on the warm side. Paige was dressed in a soft jumper for chilly weather, but all she wore was a thin t-shirt and jeans.

Down the road Tiffany didn't see any sign of houses or oncoming traffic, and on the route she'd taken, there wasn't a house in miles. *We can't just stand here and pray someone comes. Maybe if I bundle Paige up, we can find a house up the road.* Moving to the rear of her SUV, she grabbed her diaper bag out of the trunk, as well as the quilt Natalie had made for the crib.

Gently lifting Paige from the car seat, she bundled her in the quilt, careful not to disturb her. Making their way down the road would be easier if she slept. Diaper bag over her shoulder, Tiffany lifted Paige into her arms, only to nearly drop her when someone cleared his throat behind her.

"Ma'am, are you in need of assistance?"

Turning around, she found a man, and was startled by the sudden presence. She hadn't heard a car. Looking around, she realized why. There wasn't a car. "Where did you come from?" she asked, an uneasy knot forming in her stomach.

"In general or just now?" the sarcastic tone to his voice apparent.

"Now?" *Who is this man? In a small town like this, everyone knows everyone. I've never seen him.*

"I was out for a walk. You looked as though you were having car problems. I might be able to help, but if you have no interest then I'll be on my way." He turned as if ready to stroll back into the woods.

He stood before her in faded blue jeans and a light gray t-shirt. His short hair shaved close to the scalp. *Short sleeves? In this weather?*

"My car broke down. I don't know what's wrong with it. It started making a weird clicking noise a few miles ago then just died on me. Do you have a cell phone with service? I can call a tow truck."

"No service here. Let me look, maybe I can fix it."

She started to follow him to the front of the SUV when Paige began to cry. "Shh, baby. It's okay." She rocked her gently, rubbing small circles on her back, while he looked under the hood. Each second Paige's cries grew more forceful.

"Is she okay?" the man asked, coming to stand on the side of the truck again.

"She's hungry. How's my car?"

"I can fix it. I think it will start now but won't go far. You won't make it back to town with it like it is." He looked slightly uneasy, watching her and the baby. "I'm staying a little way from here. The tools I'd need to fix it should be in the garage. It should get us to my place, where I can fix it for you. It'll take an hour or two, and there's no use in you standing out here in the cold with the child."

"I can't have you do that. I'll call a tow," she hollered over Paige's cries.

"Either way you'll have to come back to the cabin. It's the only place around with service. Unless you want to wait here."

"I don't know you…I mean, you're not from around here. I know most people around here, and those I don't know I've seen around at least. I work—or should say used to work, I'm on maternity leave—at Doctor Bradley's office." She was rambling but she was unable to stop the words from seeping out.

"I'll be. Good old Doc Bradley is still practicing." He chuckled. "I grew up here, and my brothers still live here. I just got out of the Marines and am moving back. I'm sure you know Damon and Josh Andrews."

"Oh…." She switched Paige to her other shoulder. "You must be Mason then. I ran into Aspyn the other day, and she mentioned you were returning. Everyone's happy to have you back home safely. Especially with the wedding and babies."

"I mean you no harm. If you'd prefer, I'm sure either Aspyn or Damon would give you a lift back to your house, or let you stay with them if you'd prefer not to be alone with me. Either way, you and the child need to get out of the cold before you both come down sick."

"Paige—her name's Paige." She looked back at the SUV. "You sure it's safe to drive?"

"It'll be fine just going down the road. I'm staying at Aspyn's father's old cabin. It's not far."

Opening the back door, she tossed the diaper bag onto the floor before putting Paige back in her car seat. As the car seat buckle clicked home, she hollered, "Let's go then."

"Ahh, I don't want to get grease marks all over the steering wheel. Do you have any paper towels or something?"

"Better." She dug through the diaper bag. "Baby wipes. They clean up almost anything." She handed him a couple.

As he used the wipes to clean his hands, her lips curled into a smile. His black t-shirt pulled tightly over his muscles. Men with tight, toned bodies put her in turmoil. She was drawn to them, wanting to run her hands over them to feel them constrict underneath her fingers. But Paige's father showed her just how dangerous a man could be.

The man before her was trained to kill, making him deadlier than her ex, yet there was something about him that hinted to her they'd be safe with him.

Chapter Three

Mason was under the hood of the SUV, grease covering his hands, when the garage door banged closed. Lifting his head, he saw Tiffany standing in the doorframe with a mug of something in her hand.

"I hope you don't mind I made a cup of tea. I couldn't shake the chill."

He shook his head no. "I told you to make yourself at home. Shouldn't you be in there with your dau…Paige?" His didn't want to be rude, but he wasn't sure how to handle her. More than a year ago when he was home on leave, he'd seen her through the doctor's office window and she'd run through his thoughts all this time.

The mate his body and beast wanted to claim, but he refused. She deserved better than him. The baggage he had… no woman deserved to have to live with it. He would keep his distance and fight the mating. She was human and would find someone else. He, on the other hand, would lose his chance at happiness, but that was the road he chose when he joined the military.

She raised her hand, shaking a white walkie-talkie sort of devise. "Baby monitor. I'll hear her. She's asleep on your bed surrounded by the pillows. Hope you don't mind. Can I do anything to help?"

"No. I need a part." He looked up at the clock on the wall. "Bob's Auto is closed. It'll have to wait until tomorrow. I have Aspyn's Trailblazer. I borrowed it to allow me to pick up a few things in town I need tomorrow and then go shopping for a new vehicle. I sold mine when I deployed." He swallowed the lump that formed in his throat. "I can give you a lift home, and while I'm out tomorrow I'll get the part. I'll have it fixed tomorrow evening, and I'll bring it to you."

"That would be great, if you don't mind. But I could still call a tow truck if you'd prefer." She held the mug close to her chest with both hands, as if wanting to draw all of the heat from the glass.

"No use doing that. The job's almost complete, and the garage would charge you for the whole thing, plus it's a big tow expensive from way out here. If you don't mind being without the car for the night, I'll get it fixed and bring it to you once it's done."

Grabbing a rag from the workbench, he wiped most of the grease off his hands. For the first time since his military discharge, he felt almost normal. He enjoyed tinkering with cars. *Damon mentioned old man Miller was selling his garage. Maybe I should look into that. It would be something to occupy my time, and this town needs an honest mechanic.* He put it aside to think on later. "Let me wash up and I'll transfer the car seat."

Tiffany left out a heavy sigh as cries filled the small space. "Sorry for the constant cries. She's coming down with something." She moved toward the door, passing within inches of him. It took the control Mason learned in the Marines not to grab her. His animal craved her touch. "If you could put my travel bag from the trunk in your car also, please. I'll need it."

Keeping his distance, he followed her out of the garage into the cold fall air and into the house before they went their separate ways. He'd wash up in the kitchen while Tiffany went to the bedroom to the crying baby.

Do babies always cry this often? It had been years since he was around a child, let alone an infant. *Where was the baby's father?* He didn't see a ring on Tiffany's finger, but that didn't mean much nowadays. Women were having children on their own. Some by choice and others left to deal with the child when the father wasn't ready.

His animal's anger clawed at him as he thought of his mate having a child to another man. If only he would have claimed her all those years ago, that child would be his.

* * *

Alone in her home she realized she had formula for Paige but as far as real food went, the refrigerator was mostly empty. Inside set a bottle of wine, a dozen or so bottles of water, and a few cans of soda. She'd cleaned it out three weeks ago when she'd gone to her sister's.

The freezer was full, but she was too tired to pull something out. Instead, she grabbed a box of crackers off the shelf and shuffled toward her bedroom. Every part of her body was heavy, she could barely lift her legs, and her eyes were at half-mast. She was exhausted.

Sleep was what she needed, especially since Paige was finally asleep, but her stomach rumbled. She grabbed a cracker and nibbled it as she crawled into bed with Mason on her mind.

What happened to cause the deep sadness in his eyes?

Chapter Four

"Miller," Mason called pulling into Miller's Garage, "got a minute?" Putting the SUV in park, he stepped out.

"Mason. It's good to see you around these parts again. I got all the time you need. Something wrong with Aspyn's car?" He tilted his head toward the SUV in the parking lot.

"Oh no, it's fine. Damon mentioned you were selling up. Retiring. I never thought I'd see the day you let this place go."

"That's the plan, but no one's interested in the place. At least not to keep it as a garage. Had an offer from some big shot who wants to tear it down and put a four-star dining place in. I can't see that lasting long in our town. The Mrs. and I talked it over and agreed not to sell unless we find someone who'll keep it open." Miller wiped his hands on his overalls, not that it did any good. His hands needed a serious scrubbing to get the grease off them.

"I wanna buy it." He leaned against the building, watching the two guys Miller had working for him.

"What are you going to do with it? You can't run a business if you're never here."

"My brothers didn't tell you that I'm out of the Marines? My shoulder was injured while I was deployed. I'm home for good."

"Still, why the garage?"

"I've always enjoyed tinkering with cars. When one of our Humvees broke down I was the one who repaired it. I might not have been working in the garage my whole life like you and the men in there, but I know my way around a car." He slid his hands into the front pockets of his jeans and eyed Miller. "You know as well as I do our town needs this garage. I want to see it survive. I'll give you your asking price, and you and the Mrs. can enjoy your retirement."

* * *

Tiffany paced the floor with a feverish Paige in her arms. The baby's wails did nothing to calm her nerves. She tried calling Doctor Bradley on his cell phone, but he wasn't answering. *He's probably doing rounds at the hospital.* Without a car and no one to call, she was stuck until Mason arrived with her SUV. *He's got to be here soon.* She looked at the clock for the hundredth time.

Paige wouldn't eat or sleep. Tiffany had been up with the crying baby most of the night and throughout the day.

Her nerves were frazzled. The worst part of motherhood was when your child was hurting and you could do nothing to ease the pain.

"Oh darling, if I knew what would make you feel better, I'd do it." She rubbed small circles up and down her back.

When the doorbell rang, it was a heavenly sound. It had to be Mason and if it wasn't, she'd get whoever it was to take her and poor Paige to the hospital. *Damn it, her car seat is with Mason.*

* * *

When Tiffany opened the door Mason could have sworn he saw tears in her eyes. "What's wrong?"

"Paige is worse. I can't get her fever to break. I called Doctor Bradley, but he's not answering his cell phone. Did you bring my car? I have to get her to the hospital."

"Come on, I'll take you."

He watched helplessly as she slid her feet into a pair of shoes. "Her diaper bag…"

He spotted the bag on the couch, along with her purse. "Get her in the car. I'll grab it." He slid past her, making his way to the bag, wondering where she put her house keys until he saw them lying on the coffee table.

He grabbed the bag and slipped her small purse inside, before snatching the keys from the table. By the time he locked the door, Tiffany had Paige in the car seat.

"I'll drive," he hollered to her. "Maybe if you ride in the back with her, it'll help."

"Nothing helps. She hasn't stopped crying all afternoon."

He watched as she hopped into the back seat before he slid behind the wheel. "Don't worry. We'll be there in a few minutes."

He wanted to console her. To tell her everything would be fine, but he wouldn't give her false hope. He knew next to nothing about children, but his gut told him the crying wasn't normal. He didn't like to see the child suffering—it tore at his stomach like nothing he'd ever experienced.

Fifteen minutes later, he stood at the desk in the emergency room doing his best to fill out the registration forms, while Tiffany stood behind him trying to soothe Paige, who was wailing at the top of her lungs.

"I thought I heard a familiar cry. What seems to be the problem with happy–go-lucky Paige?" Doctor Bradley came out of one of the exam rooms.

"Doc, I'm so glad you're here. She's been sick the last two days, but it's been getting worse not better. Now she has a fever that won't go away. She won't eat or sleep. All she wants to do is cry."

"Come along. We'll take a look at her." The doctor turned and hit the button on the wall. The doors slid open.

Mason, not sure what else to do, followed behind helplessly.

Never in all his life had he felt this entirely helpless. He was a man of action. Give him a problem and he would find a way to fix it. This was something he couldn't fix, and it got under his skin.

Paige's cries grew louder when Tiffany laid her on the hospital bed. He watched from the corner as Tiffany cringed as the wails filled the room. Stepping forward, he wrapped his arm around her.

I shouldn't be here. I shouldn't have my arm around her. Still he couldn't force himself to leave. His mate—she was still his mate even if he hadn't claimed her—needed him. He wouldn't desert her when she was in need.

Doctor Bradley examined Paige, checking her temperature before listening to her chest intently. "I'll give her something to help with the fever and make her more comfortable. I want to run a few tests."

"What's wrong with my daughter?"

"I want to do a chest X-ray and blood work to confirm, but it sounds like a nasty chest cold. She's also dehydrated, so we'll give her an IV with fluids. With some medication, she'll be fine. I just want to make sure it doesn't turn into pneumonia. The nurse will be in shortly to give her something."

As Doctor Bradley left, Mason watched Tiffany's strength dissipate, and her knees buckled. His grip was the only thing keeping her on her feet.

"Tiff, come sit down." He directed her to the hardback chair next to the bed.

"Pneumonia," she whispered her voice cracking.

"It's just a chest cold. Don't go borrowing trouble. She's going to be fine." He ran his hand up and down her arm. "Everything is going to be fine."

"Ms. Tyler," the nurse said, entering the room. "I'm here to set up the IV and draw blood. The doctor ordered something to break the fever. It should be brought up by the time I'm finished."

"I don't know how you'll do it but go ahead. She won't quit crying. I've tried everything." The little girl's breaths were ragged from the state she'd worked herself into.

"Do you want to take a break? Go get a cup of coffee or something while…."

"No, I'm staying with my daughter."

The nurse nodded before going about her business, prepping the IV.

"Mary, here's the medication."

"Good. This little girl has worked herself into such a state, not to mention her poor mamma." She grabbed the syringe from the other woman. "This should only take a few minutes to work. It'll probably put her to sleep, which is what she needs." Taking a firm hold of Paige's chubby arm, she wiped the area with an alcohol cloth before she eased the needle home with the expertise acquired from years of experience.

"She'll calm shortly," the nurse said before slipping out the door.

The IV was dripping slowly as Paige calmed. Her sobs turned into soft whimpers.

"Tiffany…" When she didn't acknowledge him, he knelt beside the chair. "Tiff, she's going to be fine."

She sat there staring at her little girl with tears in her eyes. She smoothed the hair away from Paige's face.

"Tiff, look at me." He took his forefinger and softly moved her head to look at him. "You okay?"

"I was just thinking…." Tears now freely fell down her cheek. "I don't know what I would do without her. Beside my sister Natalie and Mom, she's all I have. My life revolves around her."

"You're not going to lose her. We're going to make sure she's okay. I promise."

Gram always said don't make promises you can't keep. I'll keep this promise. I want to take the pain from Tiffany's eyes, and if I never hear Paige cry like that again, it'll be too soon.

As Fate Would Have It

Chapter Five

Tiffany dozed in the chair next to the bed while they waited for the IV to finish its cycle. It had been a long night for everyone involved. Throughout the night Tiffany had told him to go home so many times that he lost count. How could he just leave her?

He wasn't an uncaring bastard that could leave a woman—his mate. *Damn it, I don't want a mate. I couldn't protect my men—why give me a mate I won't be able to keep safe? I can't bear to lose another.*

"Mason, you're still here?" her voice heavy with sleep as she rubbed her eyes with her thumb and forefinger.

He knelt next to her chair, taking her hand in his. "I told you I wouldn't leave."

"I'm sorry I fell asleep. You should have gone home. I'm sure you're exhausted."

"You needed your rest. Sleep while you can. I'll be here." He felt drawn to kiss her. To taste her lips on his. Before he could act on it Doctor Bradley and the nurse who started the IV walked in.

"Mary tells me Paige is doing much better. Her fever's gone." He took his stethoscope from around his neck and listened to Paige's chest. "She looks pinker, and her chest sounds a little better. It's going to take a few days, but she'll be fine. I'm going to write you a prescription, and I want to call me if things don't continue to improve. But as long as she's feeling better by the end of the week, there's no need to bring her in. I'll see her for her regular checkup the beginning of the month."

"Thank you, Doctor Bradley."

He nodded and turned to Mason. "Take good care of them." He turned toward the door, while Mary removed the IV. "Mason, I hear you're buying out Old Man Miller."

"I forgot how quickly news travels in a small town." His lips curled into a smile. "Yeah, I talked to him today. We've got an appointment with the lawyer to deal with the paperwork early next week. I'll take over the shop the beginning of the month."

"I'm glad to see you're going to settle down back home. Congratulations. The town depends on that garage."

"I have no plans for anything to change. Well maybe a fresh coat of paint. It will still be there for years to come."

Doctor Bradley left to write the prescription, and Tiffany turned to him. "You bought Miller's garage?"

"Yeah. Fixing your car reminded me how much I loved it. I need something to keep me occupied now. It seemed like the perfect fit."

"Why didn't you tell me?"

"I wanted to ask you to dinner to celebrate when I arrived at your house." The realization that he was disappointed they didn't make the dinner sank in. *What am I doing? I'm supposed to be distancing myself from her, not forcing us together.*

"I'm sorry." The tears she had held finally fell.

"Hey now, there's no need to cry. We can have dinner another night, once Paige is feeling better."

"I always ruin everything. This was supposed to be a happy day for you and instead you spent the night in the ER with me and Paige. I'm sorry."

"Tiff, you didn't ruin anything. I bought a business, not make the first trip to Mars. Paige is more important than celebrating a purchase." He put his hands on her arms, pulling her up so she was standing. Wrapping his arms around her, he held her until her tears died away.

"I'm sorry…I'm not normally a crier." She pulled back slightly so she could look up at him.

"There's no need to apologize."

Her lips were right there, begging him to claim them. Throwing caution to the wind, he tilted and lowered his head and kissed her. The sweet taste of her lips drew him in, making him want more.

With one simple kiss, his desire for her grew, making it harder now for him to deny she was his. But what if he couldn't keep her safe?

Chapter Six

*What the hell was I thinking kissing her? Is the heartache I caused
my men's widows not enough? I don't need to ruin another life. When
will I ever learn? It is better to be alone than to lose someone.* He
wanted to kick himself for his stupidity.

The sun was peeking over the horizon when they final
pulled in front of Tiffany's house. He looked around for
the truck he bought when it dawned on him that yesterday
at his arrival, he'd driven her SUV. *Shit. It's going to be a long
walk home this morning.*

"Take the car. I'd take you home, but I'm not sure I
can keep my eyes open enough to drive," she told him as if
she read his mind.

"No need. I'll walk."

"Mason, it's ten miles. Take the car and get some rest.
When you bring it back, we can have dinner to celebrate.
I'll cook."

"There's no need…"

"There is. Let me make dinner for you after all you did. Say seven o'clock or is that too late? I'll have Paige fed and in bed, and we can enjoy dinner."

There were a dozen reasons why he shouldn't, but he couldn't help himself. The thought of having dinner with her was too tempting. "I'll be here. Can I bring anything?"

"Just yourself." He looked toward her only to find her smiling back at him. There was a mischievous twinkle in her eyes.

* * *

After putting Paige in her crib and slipping into her lounge pants, Tiffany headed to the freezer, her thoughts centered on Mason. *He's very attractive, but what could he see in me? A man like him could have his pick of women. He doesn't want one with an infant in tow.*

She tried to push her thoughts away from him. Telling herself she only offered to cook dinner to thank him for his help, not because she was attracted to him. But the tingle between her thighs and the hardening of her nipples suggested differently.

She pulled out a package of chicken breasts to thaw. She'd make grilled chicken marsala with pasta for dinner. It was something she could cook in her sleep, so it wouldn't let her down. She wanted something delicious yet she couldn't mess up. No new recipes on a night like this.

With food planned, she had to worry about clothes. Staring at her clothes, she felt disappointed by the options. *I want something that will show him I'm not just a mother but also a woman. A woman with desires.* And right now she desired him.

* * *

"You look exhausted. Where have you been? Whose car?"

Mason forced his body out of the driver's seat as Damon interrogated him. It had been years since someone besides his commanding officer demanded to know where he was. He was a grown man with no one to answer to, not even his C.O.

"I am exhausted. I've been up since early yesterday morning." He ran his hand over his face, the five o'clock shadow rugged against his hand, as he ignored the other questions. He didn't want to talk about Tiff. "What are you doing here?"

"You didn't answer my questions. I heard in town you are buying out Old Man Miller's. I thought you might come work with Josh and me."

"I've never been one for construction work. You know that. I don't have the woodworking talent you have, or the eye for design like Josh. Cars are my thing. I hope you'll both be supportive." He was tired and had no patience for this conversation.

"Whatever makes you happy, we're behind you. Now are you going to answer my questions?"

Mason made the few steps to the porch before collapsing. "It's Tiffany Tyler's vehicle. She broke down not far from here a couple days ago. I was fixing it. When I went to return it yesterday, her daughter was extremely ill. I've been at the hospital with her all night. Now if you're satisfied, I'd like to get some sleep. I promised I'd take it back to her tonight."

Damon's nostrils flared seconds before his eyes widened. "You've found your mate."

It wasn't a question, more of a statement, but still Mason felt the need to deny it. "I don't know what you're talking about." He forced himself to stand. "I'm going to get some sleep. If you want to spend your time sitting here, be my guest."

"Mason, if you've never taken advice from Josh and me before, take this. Don't fight it. It'll only make the mating stronger. I know Tiffany quite well. She already knows about our kind. Talk to her. Don't push her away." With that, he shifted and took off toward his house, leaving only the shreds of his clothes behind.

She knows about our kind. How?

Chapter Seven

Damon's words continued to replay in Mason's thoughts on the drive to Tiffany's. *What did he mean she knows about our kind?* Surely, his brothers or future sister-in-laws didn't blab their secret to an outsider. Being a shifter was a closely guarded secret. To tell someone gave them the power not only to ruin you but your family and all shifters. It was a power rarely given to anyone but their mates.

When he got out of the SUV, he was still trying to figure how he could ask Tiff what she knew about shifters and give his secret away. *She's your mate—she wouldn't betray you if she knew. No, I can't claim her as my mate.*

The turmoil he was in fell away when she opened the door. She stood before him in black leggings and a light blue sweater. Her brown wavy hair hung loose around her face. Casually leaning against the doorframe, she took his breath away. *Imagine coming home every night to this and the beautiful little girl.*

"I'm glad you could make it."

"I wouldn't miss it. Plus it will be nice to have a home-cooked meal. I haven't had one in a long time."

She chuckled. "No pressure."

"None at all. I'm sure you're a great cook. Even if you're mediocre, it's better than the military food and a hundred times better than anything I try to make. I'm a disaster in the kitchen." Now standing in front of her, he wanted to kiss her. His body stiff with the desire, but he pushed it away.

"Come in. Dinner's almost done." She turned and strolled through the living room, toward the back of the house. He could see the kitchen archway and the refrigerator.

She left him no choice but to follow or stand in the doorway. He shut the door behind him before following her.

The kitchen was updated recently. The light golden granite counters shone against the dark cherry wood cabinets. There was a small dining table at the far end of the kitchen, where a bottle of wine sat open breathing.

"I opened a bottle of wine. If you don't want any, I have soda and water. Sorry I can't offer you a beer or anything stronger."

She stood by the kitchen sink, looking nervous. He went to her, not touching but close enough that if either moved their bodies would meet. "Don't be nervous." He lowered his head and kissed her.

Their kiss broke, and she sighed, her shoulders relaxing. "I'm glad you're here."

"Me too." He wrapped his arms around her, pressing his body into hers, until she was up against the counter.

The oven beeped, he assumed signaling the garlic bread that he smelled was ready. "Dinner's ready."

He stepped back. "What can I do?"

"Grab the bread from the oven and put it on the table please. I'll bring the rest." She grabbed a large serving bowl from the overhead cabinet and put the pasta into it before adding the sauce and chicken she cut into strips. She took the tongs and mixed everything together before placing it on the table.

Mason had two glasses of wine poured before she sat down and had already begun to dish the pasta onto the plates.

"Why did you leave the Marines?"

Mention of the Marines always brought back the memories of his last mission, followed by the guilt. "Our last mission went wrong. My arm was injured...I had no choice."

"I'm sorry. I didn't know. Your brothers were so proud of you, but you could tell they missed you. I'm sure they're happy to have you back."

"I guess. I know Damon is disappointed I won't be joining them in the family business. I should have told them before I spoke with Miller, but what's done is done." He took a large mouthful of the pasta and chicken. "Delicious."

"It's a family recipe Mom passed down to me. One of my favorite dishes. I hope you don't mind chicken instead of some red meat. My..."

"Not at all. I love chicken. Your what?" he said between mouthfuls.

"Paige's father preferred steak. I guess during our...time...together I got tired of steak."

He set his fork down and focused on her. "Since you brought him up. Is he, um, in the picture still? Does he help you with her?"

"He's no longer with us. He passed away while I was pregnant. It's just me and Paige now."

He could see the sadness in her eyes. "Oh Tiff. I'm sorry."

"Thank you. It's the reason Natalie and Mom are nagging me to come stay with them. I just can't sell my home and leave. I was on my way back from visiting them when I broke down."

No ring on her finger, no husband, no father for Paige. He couldn't just walk away from them. He couldn't claim her as his mate, but he could do what he could for her until she found another man.

* * *

Dinner was wonderful. Great food, better company, and even little Paige decided to make a visit. Holding Paige earlier made him realize he was already in too deep with Tiff, and he was enjoying every minute of it. He never got around to asking her how she knew about shifters. It never seemed like the right time—at least that's what he kept telling himself—but somehow he thought it was because he wasn't sure he wanted to know the answer.

He had always been a loner but on his way home, he felt lonelier than ever before in his life. He missed Tiff. His body craved her touch, his thoughts revolved around her, he wanted to spend every moment with her.

When turning onto the country road that would lead him home, there was a truck parked across the road. This route was traveled often now that there was a new highway, but it was still the only way to his cabin. *What's going on here?* Chance, one of the lone wolves from the mountain, leaned against the truck.

"Chance, what's going on? Did you break down?" Mason hollered, pulling Tiff's SUV to a stop. He'd ended up driving the SUV home again instead of disturbing Paige, with the idea they'd go to lunch tomorrow and then she could drop him off at his house and take the SUV home.

"Just need a moment of your time and I'll move the truck."

Weird. "What can I do for you?"

"More like that I can do for you." Chance stalked toward Mason. "That woman killed before. Stay away from Tiffany Tyler unless you want to end up like my brother."

Mason was shocked. How could someone believe Tiff could kill someone, let alone a male shifter? Before he could question Chance, he was back in his truck and driving away. Mason pulled his cell phone out of the cup holder. He was still close enough to town to pick up cell service. Punching in Damon's number, he pulled the SUV to the shoulder.

When his brother answered, he jumped right to the point. "What's Tiffany's past? How does she know of shifters?"

Outside the window, the trees were full of color. The leaves littered the ground, while squirrels and chipmunks gathered their nuts for the upcoming winter. "I just left her place, but I didn't ask her. How was that supposed to come up in regular dinner conversation?"

A deer stood at the edge of the woods taking note of his stopped car before it scurried across the road. "I didn't give much thought about it until Chance was waiting for me on my way home." He paused while Damon asked about the encounter. "It was a warning of sorts. Mentioned something about how she killed his brother. What the hell does that mean? Tiff couldn't kill someone, especially not a shifter."

When Damon was no help, he tossed the phone onto the passenger's seat and turned the SUV around. He wanted—no he needed—answers. Tiff was the only one who could give him the answers he needed.

As Fate Would Have It

Chapter Eight

Tiffany was putting the last of the dinner dishes in the dishwasher when her doorbell rang. *Who could that me? Perhaps Mason forgot something.*

Sure enough, she opened her door to find Mason standing there. The air around him seemed charged. She could tell he was upset, but the reason behind such a mood change was beyond her.

"What's wrong, Mason?"

"Can we talk?"

"Sure. Come in." She moved aside to give him room to pass. When he stood in her living room, she asked, "What's on your mind? You seem angry."

"I had an encounter with Chance on my way home…."

She could feel the color drain from her face, and she felt suddenly sick. *Not Chance.*

"From your expression I take it you know him. Good, since what he had to say tonight concerns you."

"I can explain," she whispered, not sure how but she'd do her best. She sank to the couch, her legs too weak to keep her standing.

"Go on then." He took a seat on the chair, giving her the impression he didn't want to be close.

"Chance's brother Trace was Paige's father." He voice cracked. She never told anyone, not even her sister that Trace was the father. She'd found out she was pregnant a few weeks after his death, and by that time Chance was already blaming her. She wouldn't have her daughter forced into the situation where she had to listen to Chance's lies or defend her mother. To Tiffany it was best to deny she was his daughter.

"Then you know what he was, what his family is?"

"Yes, they're shifters. Trace told me. We were supposed to marry, before his death."

"Why does Chance believe you killed his brother?"

There was the dreaded question. "I guess in a way I'm responsible for it." She ran her hand through her hair and took a deep breath. "We had an argument. He wanted me to give up my job, sell the house and move to the mountain with him. But his family considered me an outsider, and I never felt comfortable there. I couldn't live on the mountain surrounded by them day in and day out.

He was upset with me and took off for a run. The neighbor, Jason, down the road saw a wolf and shot him."

She paused, giving him a moment to digest the information before adding, "Chance saw Jason and me in town the day before having lunch together. He concluded we were having an affair. When Trace found out about it, he shifted and went after Jason, which is how Trace ended up killed." She played with the charm on her necklace, moving it back and forth along the chain. "Nothing was going on between Jason and me. But Chance and his family didn't believe me."

For the first time she was able to get it off her chest and a feeling of relief came over her. She'd never told anyone the full story. No one would have believed her if she had. Normal people don't know about shifters. If she started going on about people shifting into wolves, they'd have committed her, then were would her daughter be?

Mason's silence had her nerves on edge. She expected him to storm off, not just sit there. "I understand if you don't believe me and want nothing more to do with us. The news of shifters is a lot to take in."

"Tiff…" He moved to the couch and took a seat beside her. "I believe you."

"I know it sounds crazy…wait, what? You believe me? About shifters? About how he died?"

He laid his hand on her leg. "I believe you. I know shifters exist. I'm a mountain lion. As for how he died, I have no reason to doubt you. You said marriage, but were you his mate?"

"It wasn't until after he died I found out more about shifters. Damon came to me after his funeral to check on me. Mates left behind normally die shortly after. When Damon came, he found that I wasn't mated. Something to do with my scent, I guess. You'd have to ask him for the details on that. The mountain wolves don't believe in mates as many of the other shifters do. They take many 'wives' to produce children. I'm not sure how they get around having children with more than one woman, or with women who are not their mates. As Damon explained it, there's normally one mate, and only that person can they have children with." She gave him a nervous smile. "I'm sorry I'm rambling. You already know about mates."

"It's fine. They get around it because the mountain wolves are not full-blooded shifters. They have been crossbreeding for so long their line is dying out. You weren't his mate, or I'd still be able to smell his scent on you." He ran his hand over her leg. "But this does make things easier. Tiff, I'm your mate."

"I don't know if I can deal with shifters again." She pulled away from him. *I have to worry about Paige, not my bloody hormones.*

"Don't hold the fact I can shift into a mountain lion against me. You know my family. We are nothing like the wolves. In the last few days you have come to know me, and you should know I'd never do anything to hurt you."

"I'm not worried about me. I can take the hurt and the heartbreak. I'm worried about Paige."

"What about Paige? She already has me wrapped about her little finger."

"What happens if she goes through the change? She'll be a wolf among a family of mountain lions."

Mason moved closer to her. "She'll be family. It won't matter what she shifts into. She'll be my daughter and you'll be my mate." His lips claimed hers.

As Fate Would Have It

Chapter Nine

Mason ran his hand through her hair as he kissed her, drawing her closer to him. The taste of the wine from earlier still lingered on her lips, making him want to drink her up. "Let me make love to you," he whispered as their kiss broke apart.

When she gave a faint nod, he lifted the light blue sweater over her head. He wouldn't give her a chance to change her mind. The sweater lay lost on the floor, and Mason kissed her neck before slowly working his way down to her breasts. He drew his tongue along the tops of her breasts where the cups of the bra hid the best part from view, as he slipped his hands around back to unhook her bra.

Mason leaned over her, claiming her lips again, before kissing a path down her body, spending extra time for each breast. As he kissed her abdomen, he slid his fingers beneath the elastic waistband of her leggings and pulled them down her legs.

He lifted himself off her to strip away his own clothes. Tossing them on the floor, he looked down at Tiff lying naked on the couch. The soft light from the fire reflecting off her skin matched the heat they both felt.

"You're beautiful." He watched as her cheeks reddened with embarrassment.

He slid on top of her, taking hold of her nipple with his mouth. Teasing it with his tongue, causing her to arch her back under him. He caressed each inch of her body.

He placed his hands gently on her knees, spreading them, giving him the access that he desired. He slid his shaft into her wet core just as his animal had begged him to do since he laid eyes on her. The air around them began to warm and sizzle.

"What's that?" she asked is a husky voice.

"It's normal."

Their bodies, bound together, found rhythm as passion vibrated through them, seeking release. Waves of ecstasy engulfed them, making him roar. Tiff squirmed beneath him, arching her back as her climaxed neared. Her hands dug into his shoulders as she pulled him closer. Their lips meeting again as they both reached their peaks. As release overcame him, he broke the kiss, leaned his head back and roared.

He paused, listening to hear if his roar woke Paige, but the baby monitor stayed silent, indicating she was sleeping heavily still. He used the last of his energy and strength to roll them both over, allowing her to lie on top of him.

"What are you doing?"

"I'm too heavy to lay on you, and there's not enough room beside you. I want to feel your body against mine."

* * *

Hours later Mason woke to find himself in her bed with Tiff snuggled against him. His arm tight around her as if his unconscious mind was afraid to lose her. Sometime doing the night, they'd made love again before finally finding enough energy to make it to her bed.

He laid there wondering if mating with Tiff was the worst decision he'd made. Careful not to move, he watched her sleep. *Will I ruin her life like I ruined my men's widows?*

Her eyes popped open. "Mason, what's wrong? I can feel your pain."

Shit.

"It's nothing. Go back to sleep."

"Talk to me. Why am I feeling this? I know what I'm feeling isn't my own."

He ran his finger across her cheek. "Mating allows you to know your mate inside and out."

"Then tell me why you're in so much pain. Help me understand what we're feeling. It feels endless—there's so much sadness and heartache." She ran her hand over his chest.

"I'm sorry, Tiff. I didn't mean for you to have to go through this. I wasn't thinking when I mated you."

"Are you saying you regret it?" she asked, pulling away from him and taking the sheet with her.

"Yes. I mean no. Oh Tiff…this is coming out wrong."

She jumped out of bed, wrapping the sheet around her body. "I think you should leave."

"Tiff, hear me out." He went to her, not caring he was naked, and put his hand on her arm. "Just sit down and listen to me." He guided her to the bed, surprised she let him. "Everything I do is wrong. I've ruined lives. You deserve more than a screw-up. You deserve someone without a trail of damaged lives behind him, someone who can give you everything you want and more."

"What if I want you? I don't know what has caused you so much heartache or why you feel unworthy, but I can't help you if you won't talk to me. You're the one I want, the one we need. You've proven yourself worthy of us. Don't destroy it because you have doubts."

"Tiff, you don't understand…"

"You're damn right I don't understand, because you won't tell me. You're keeping me in the dark. Closing me out. Don't do this, Mason." She laid her hand on his leg as he knelt in front of her. "Don't push me away. I can help you. Whatever it is, we'll get through it together."

He stood, moving away from her, to stare out the open window. The rain came in throughout the night, taking the remaining leaves off the trees, leaving them bare like he would be when he told her.

"I was leading the last mission in Afghanistan. Everything was going according to plan until Jamieson left his cover to rescue a young child. The minute he left his cover, the gunfire started. Jamieson was riddled with bullets, but somehow the child survived. He saved that child's life but at the cost of his. He had a wife and newborn at home…" He paused as the memories played before him like a bad dream. "When everything ended I'd lost over half of my men, and a couple others were seriously injured."

"That's when you were injured?"

He nodded. "I was closest to Jamieson's position. I attempted to get him and the child out of harm's way while my men tried to cover us. I was shot in the leg and arm. My leg healed fine, and in time my shoulder will too. But the military discharged me since humans would never regain full movement in their arm. It doesn't matter. That gunfight took away more than my career. It took away men I trained, trusted. It left widows in its wake." His fists balled at his sides. He wanted to punch something. "I couldn't save my men. You deserve someone who can protect you."

She rose, easing close to him slowly. When she neared him, she put her hand on his back. "Mason, that wasn't your fault. It was war. You can't beat yourself up about this. The lives lost will forever be in your memory, as they should, but you can't give up living."

"You deserve...."

"Don't give me that line that I deserve someone better. Even if I wanted someone else, which I don't, it's too late. We mated."

Chapter Ten

Will Mason run out on us now? Are we too much for him to handle? Tiffany wondered as she fed Paige. Mason had left an hour ago to return home to shower and change. When he left, he kissed her and Paige goodbye and said he'd be back shortly. She could only hope.

"Will Mason and the Andrews family accept you as one of their own, or will you always be an outcast?" she said to Paige, not expecting an answer. She prayed Paige would find the love of a family with the Andrews, and a father in Mason.

Mason told Tiffany she deserved everything she wanted and more, but to her it was Paige who deserved it all. Her daughter was innocent in the mess she created. Trace could have never been the father Paige deserved or the husband Tiffany wanted. But Mason could be.

Her worries of Mason returning vanished when she heard someone pull into the driveway. *Mason.* She got up from the kitchen table. Setting the bottle on the counter, she walked to the window. Her SUV was parked there along with two other trucks.

She pulled opened the door with the hand that wasn't holding Paige. "Mason, what's going on?"

"I had Damon follow with my truck, and Aspyn's in his to take him home. Stay inside—we'll be in soon. Just got to grab a few things."

Not wanting Paige to get sick again, she turned to put the baby in the bassinet near the fireplace. Paige was a good baby, sleeping through most of the night, and rarely fussed unless she was under the weather. Since the hospital visit, the antibiotics were working and she was feeling better.

Mason and Damon came in, their arms loaded with bags. "What's all that?"

"Food. I made Aspyn go shopping with me so it's not all microwavable or junk food," Mason said on his way through to the kitchen.

"I promise there's some good food in there," Aspyn said, following the men in and laughing. "I'm not sure we actually met, but I'm Aspyn, Damon's mate."

"Tiffany, and that's Paige."

Aspyn looked in the bassinet at Paige. "She's adorable. How old?"

"She'll be twelve weeks this weekend."

"I better go help the men or your fridge will be an unorganized mess." The women went into the kitchen. Tiffany was putting the canned goods in the pantry when Paige started to fuss. *Diaper change.*

"I got her. I missed my sweetie pie." Mason dropped what he had in his hand back onto the counter.

"I think she needs a diaper change. I'll get her."

"I think Paige and I can manage. We'll holler if you're needed." He already had her in his arms and headed towards the nursery.

What happened to him between this morning and now?

* * *

This was the life. Paige was asleep in his arm, while Tiff was curled up next to him, his other arm around her.

"What happened while you were gone? You came back with a peace you didn't have."

"I talked to Damon. We've always been close, and he gave me the kick in the ass I needed. I won't let the best thing that happened to me go by."

"The best thing that happened to you?"

"You and Paige." He kissed her forehead. "You're my mate. My past isn't something I'm proud of, but if you can accept the man it has made me into, then we can put it behind us and be the family I want. I love you, Tiffany Tyler. Marry me."

"If you can accept my past and Paige as your own daughter then yes, I'll marry you. I love you."

"This beautiful girl owns my heart. I love her as if she was my own."

Chapter Eleven

Eight Months Later...

Mason stood in the garden, surrounded by family.
Damon and Aspyn and Josh and Sarah had just welcomed
their new daughters into the family a week ago. Mason was
surprised not only at how close the two friends were—
having a double wedding and their daughters being born
only minutes apart—but that they welcomed Tiff into their
sisterhood circle immediately. The three couples spent a
few evenings a week together. Tiffany had her house on
the market and they were building one on the far side of
the pond where Aspyn's father's cabin once stood. It
would be completed in a month's time.

Mason caught his wife's eye. She was sitting on a
blanket with Paige. In a few weeks they would be
celebrating Paige's first birthday. She was an active child,
always on the move. They agreed not to shelter her from

his animal. He shifted in front of her, getting her used to his other form.

"Little brother, you look deep in thought," Damon said, coming to stand next to him, beer in hand.

"I was thinking of how everything changed."

"Fate delivered you the family that you didn't know you wanted. There's nothing better than that."

Damon's words hit home. For years he fought mating with every fiber of his being, but now he couldn't imagine his life without Tiff and Paige. Fate always got its way.

ABOUT THE AUTHOR

Born and raised in the Pittsburgh, Pennsylvania area, Marissa Dobson now resides about an hour from Washington, D.C. She is a lady who likes to keep busy, and is always busy doing something. With two different college degrees, she believes you are never done learning.

Being the first daughter to an avid reader, this gave her the advantage of learning to read at a young age. Since learning to read she has always had her nose in a book. It wasn't until she was a teenager that she started writing down the stories she came up with.

Marissa is blessed with a wonderful supportive husband, Thomas. He is her other half and allows her to stay home and pursue her writing. He puts up with all her quirks and listens to her brainstorm in the middle of the night?

Her writing buddies Max (a cocker spaniel) and Dawne (a beagle mix) are always around to listen to me bounce ideas off them. They might not be able to answer, but they are helpful in their own ways.

She love to hear from readers so send her an email at marissa@marissadobson.com or visit her website www.marissadobson.com

Other Books by Marissa Dobson

Tiger Time

The Tiger's Heart

Snowy Fate

Sarah's Fate

Mason's Fate

Learning to Live

Passing On

Restoring Love

Winterbloom

Secret Valentine

The Twelve Seductive Days of Christmas

CPSIA information can be obtained at www.ICGtesting.com
Printed in the USA
LVOW11s1851250515

439714LV00001B/133/P